The UnValentine Anthology

By Filidh Publishing Authors

Copyright 2014 Zoe Duff

All rights reserved.

Filidh Publishing, Victoria, BC

ISBN 978-0-9813065-6-8 (Soft Cover)
Revised, 2021
Edited by Diane Cliffe

Cover Design by Zoe Duff & Danny Weeds

Proceeds of sale of this book are donated to PEERS Victoria.

Mission Statement: "PEERS is a non-profit society established by former sex workers and community supporters and is dedicated to the empowerment, education and support of sex workers by working to improve their safety and working conditions, assisting those who desire to leave the sex industry, increasing public understanding and awareness of these issues, and promoting the experiential voice." www.safersexwork.ca

This book is a collection of unusual love stories dedicated to those who follow their hearts and find happiness in creating their own paths.

Table of Contents

AB King
    Fuzzy   8

Brianna Kempe
    Leather Bound Love   12

Jessie Blair
    Fundamental Challenges   26

Katie Horricks-King
    First Born   44
    Karma   55

Kelly Duff
    S.M.A.   66

Kristoffer Law
    Happy Anniversary   80

Monique Jacob
    First Responder   96
    Mrs. Kwan   106

Pam Desjardine

    Chance Encounter — 112

Peninah Rost

    Beyond Ornately Carved Doors — 118

Ron Kearse

    The Snow Falls on Montreal — 144

S.M. King

    Vide Cor Meum — 170

Thomas Keesman

    The Farmer Takes a Wife — 184

Vince Galati

    A Dream Infernal — 208

Zoe Duff

    The Lady and the Adventurer — 230

    Multi-faceted Love — 236

About Filidh Publishing Authors — 245

AB King

In 1952 a woman of slight build managed a feat of Herculean proportions. She dumped an eight-pound mewling prat upon an unsuspecting world. A.B. King, born in the Great State of Innocence, also known as W.O. Mitchell country adapted well to his new surroundings. Vast, clear blue skies, blistering summer heat, miles of virgin prairie, a ravine with a creek, dust storms, tumbleweeds, steam locomotives, horse-drawn milk wagons, blinding snow blizzards with cold that would freeze the nuts off a steel bridge were the things of his childhood.

Adequately educated and widely read, his greatest teacher was Life itself. King loves music from many genres, reading, quiet contemplation, solitude and meaningful conversation. And puns. One mustn't leave wordplay out of it. Mr. King has experienced a lot of what life has to offer, from the sublime innocence of childhood and the ravages of the educational system to soldiering, architectural draughting, cartography, graphic arts, entrepreneurship, and much, much more. His stories are usually shorter than his biography.

Now residing in almost splendid isolation on Vancouver Island, Mr. King misses Prairie Sunsets and Thunderstorms but misses not one iota of the cold and snow. His greatest joys in life are his spawn and their spawn - Demons all, and incredible spirits each and every one of them.

Fuzzy

The time was right.

The gods decreed that the time was

right—a winter's eve.

Clear, black skies with stars that jumped out of the heavens and into my soul.

I split wood and arranged it in tiers. Piled high and with care. Going inside, I made a pot of coffee. While it brewed, I cleansed my body and then donned fresh garments. A note. A note of love was composed. I kissed her one last time and laid her softly down on her blanket. Food and other offerings were arranged around her. The note was gently placed upon her breast. I caressed her cheek once more. And ran my fingers over her golden mane. With tears welling up, I closed the lid. Pouring a coffee, I say: "Well, Fuzzy, I guess it's time." Solemnly the coffin is carried to the pyre. A match is struck and applied to wadded-up paper. It catches, the kindling catches, the fire catches and grows. Flames rise higher and higher. Orange, red, blue, yellow are the colours of the night. Thoughts flow. Tears flow. Time flows. I can see that the pyre fire has returned her body to its' elements. The same elements that make up me. The same elements that have been in existence from the beginning. Recycled how many times and in how many ways?

It's only a fire now. NO, IT'S NOT. It's not just a fire, now. There is no now. Time has no place here.

It's Fuzzy's fire. It goes on. Not done. It moves with the same frenetic energy that was her life. It dances, spins, swirls, twists, twirls. Point. With shadows playing counterpoint. It's calm, soothing, gentle, warm. Then it roars to new heights. Pops and cracks echo through the night as sparks rival the stars for brilliance and effect.

All for a hamster. No, not just for a hamster. It's all for another life. A creature that was imbued with the same life-force that dwells in us all. That dwells in all living things. Sentient or not. Flora or fauna.

It's all for another citizen of the universe.

The fire is now faded. Glowing coals and thoughts. Like the fire, Fuzzy now is now a glimmering, glowing coal in the memory of my mind.

See her shimmer. Feel the warmth.

And shed a tear.

It's all right.

Brianna Kempe

Brianna has been in love with words from a young age, and the affair got even stronger once she fled from the Political Science classroom to the writingroom her freshman year of college. She holds a Bachelor of Creative Writing from Miami University.It really just hangs on her wall.

Brianna writes when she can, balancing motherhood, working outside the home, volunteering, and the desire for a fun and fulfilling life. However, ideas are always floating around in her head. Some form of a work-in-process always keeps her on her mental toes and her fingertips from getting too soft.

Leather Bound Love

Brooke's posture whispered that she wanted to be elsewhere, which I could always hear over the chaos of five under five...the battle for the crown of the kindergartners, the middle girl - aged three "and a half thank you" - poking the younger twins with her fingers and words, and the small toddlers exploding in cries and a refusal to eat. Father would then pay unwarranted amounts of attention to the frazzled twin boys, the youngest and least able to explain their emotions. Brooke's fork scraped the plate to get all of the rice, the only audible sound coming from her seat, her concentration on dinner far too strong.

Once a meal, Father's focus would break from the boys, interrupting Brooke's long-grain chase, to ask something about school, most often having to do with literature. I could hear the cloaked gratefulness in his voice for someone to ask an intelligent question of and the pain in his silence when she would answer the question but never add to the conversation. She lurked in the shadows of personal connections and did everything she could to stay out of the spotlight. She spoke with her chin nearly touching her collarbone, never bringing her eyes up to meet another's. Even her consistent use of "sir" seemed intended to swing the attention to someone, anyone else.

Father would turn back to the youngest, his disappointment clear to Mother and eldest, and I would pay my own version of attention to Brooke. The deafening creak of her chair as she shifted her weight, aware my eyes were now on her, too, complimented the final scrape of her fork and the precise clang as she set it on her plate. I shuddered as I watched her practiced movements and wondered when she had become so adept at shutting me out.

She was not secretive about her life, how her classes were going, what she wanted to be when she grew up, what she loved, what she hated, what she thought she might like for dinner next week, but neither did she express certainty. Her response to a question started with a shrug and a nonchalant answer which always ended with a mumbled "maybe...," the ellipsis audible.

I glanced often at her, thinking of all the questions I was too afraid of a silent response to ask.

Brooke did not share stories or empathize with the stories others shared. When the twins raved about how they had been chosen to lead the school in a flag ceremony, she did not show excitement. When they told us all of the mishap with the flag and the mud puddle, a twinkle of mischievousness apparent to me in their eyes, she did not show pity, sadness, or pride, any one of which would have meant a connection, a cause for celebration in my heart.

Brooke would keep to herself throughout most of the evening schedule, heading to her attic bedroom as soon as she returned home from school, never bringing friends or asking to use the telephone. She would come down for dinner or any other time she was called, but she always maintained her distance politely. Her obedience and docility created a wall around her, unscalable.

Her disconnect was never voiced, but Brooke looked at each of us with static eyes. The only energy I could detect was an eagerness to be elsewhere. I wanted to hug her; I watched for any sign, anxious to fulfill her needs for affection, and I was always disappointed.

I might not have known much, but I knew enough. Every dinner, Brooke's focus transferred between her plate and the window. Always looking outside... I knew what that meant, myself having been a teenager wanting to escape home. I had created a circle of boyfriends who were able to whisk me away any evening I wished. I, too, had always kept my eyes on the windows, waiting to see the headlights flash, letting me know a knight in a rusty car had arrived. And now, Brooke focused outside too, ready to escape life, to or from, I was never sure which.

Teachers and other parents told me that Brooke would blossom into the beauty we all knew she was, and once she knew it too, nothing would stop her, no matter which direction she wanted to go. Everyone was sure of it.

My confidence was of a different sort. No matter the enigma she presented to everyone else, I knew my daughter was certain who she was. She was obedient to all rules of social engagement but always from the perimeter. She acted as though she was waiting for an unseen master to nod his approval to join in, and she was comfortable on the outskirts of a conversation, as though the distance completed her.

How Brooke had been able to achieve such wholeness when I had struggled for years to take a small step toward it was unclear. I wanted to be proud of her, but I struggled with pride where I felt my own failure.

In order to mask my insecurities, I would send her on her way at the end of dinner, after plates had been cleared. My heart cracked, knowing that what she wanted lay outside the home I had worked to create for her.

Escapes are not without consequence, but Brooke was a different child than I had been. Smarter, keener, more ready to grow, and so, each night, I would give her permission to liberate herself for the evening. Brooke would run to her room, grab her bag, andleave the house under the cover of the setting sun and the whirl of noises that came from her younger brothers and sisters. While she was gone, the bedtime routine would start; I bathing some children, Father reading stories to the others.

Brooke would come back after having completed some chore I had not yet thought to ask of her. The trash can might have been taken to the curb, or the recycling bin brought back to the side of the house. She would come in with a gallon of milk from the corner store, and I would belatedly realize it was needed for the bedtime ritual. Father saw only these pieces of the story, and he would smile at her return, thinking she had only the best interest of the family at heart.

In her bag, I would see evidence of a rendezvous, always just peeking out of a corner. A bit of leather binding, the tassel of a marker. The colour was a bit brighter in her cheeks, her hair more mussed than when she had left.

Brooke was growing up, and I had to accept that her escapes were far more enticing than any I had ever experienced. I had escaped out of a house into a car, never going further than a deserted parking lot.

I had never known love affairs like Brooke's, the moments of held breath at a scene that was just too perfect, the dialogue that made a heart skip a beat or two, or the flutter of eyelids when the ending became evident. Brooke always seemed to find a new love; she was never without the teeth marks on her lips that proved someone new dominated her thoughts. She had excitement and adventure, laughter and fear, often all within the limits of one night.

She would come home with an air of peace and calm that perpetuated the need to bound out nightly. When she missed a few days, due to a chill in the air or the cold in her lungs, her drop would be perceptible to all of us, though I believe I was the only one capable of making a connection between a lack of an escapade and her sudden mood swings.

I had worked to create a loving and peaceful home for my family, thinking if I provided enough love, nothing more would be sought, but Brooke defied that logic. She needed the chance to experience the colours of the world instead of the drabness of a functional kitchen and her dark bedroom. She needed to know yellows and reds, blues and grays. Restrictive guidelines, created in a void of compassion, like those I had once known intimately, would never give her that rainbow. Uncensored freedom brightened her eyes and her cheeks, making her more beautiful than when she had left.

Of course, I feared for my daughter's safety, too. We had talked about the ways in which danger could be mitigated, by choosing carefully who Brooke spent her time with, by realizing that not all suitors would be well suited to her tastes. How she could not simply look at the outward appearances to determine the worth of what was inside. How to soothe the cuts that might come to her hands and her heart from playing in the ways that she was. She wearied of these conversations over time, though I was proud I found ways to discuss these guidelines without ever telling my daughter what she could or could not do.

My mother had established a set of rules by which I was expected to live: never leave her eyesight or range of control. I had taken to sneaking out late at night and sneaking back in early in the morning, with mascara that would need to be removed before my mother saw me in the morning. I worked to escape the confines of my mother and ended up well versed in the confines of the back seat of Volkswagon Beetles.

I thought I had prepared my daughter with basic knowledge, had taught her to take care of herself, how to come home with smiles instead of tears, but a mother cannot protect against everything a child will face over the course of youth. I cursed my lack of ability when Brooke came back into the home one night, her eyes swollen from tears, her cheeks streaked red where she had tried to wipe them away with harsh and hurried movements. Brooke brushed past me in the small kitchen and made her way to the attic. It was the first time she had not bothered to supplement the outing with a ruse of helpfulness. She carried no milk, left no indication that she had gone out to get the uncollected mail.

Brooke grunted without turning when I called to say she seemed upset, hoping she would hear my concerned voice or look back to see the worry in my eyes so strong it blurred my vision.

Brooke had taken her bag with her when she pushed past, and I had been able to catch no glimpse of anything that might have been the cause of Brooke's emotional swing. If I had seen it, I don't know that I would have understood the implications.

What could I have done differently? Filled her with the ability to foresee the ending before an adventure even began? Wouldn't that knowledge take away the joy of discovery? Wasn't that the point of her explorations? Tormenting questions with no answers.

Everyone faces the consequences of their choices, and everyone must. Case in point: Me.

I had gotten pregnant. My mother had limited me

to the couch in the living room, the formal one, where the cushions were as cold and rigid as ice, so that no one would stay longer than they were welcome, never very long. The canvas curtains hid all visions of escape, blocked all stray breezes which would have broughtthe scent of cherry blossoms and peace. There, she expected me to make socks and caps, things that would keep the infant warm, though not comfortable, as she never bought soft yarn. Discomfort seemed to be the only way she knew how to live.

I knew that these restrictions would kill my heart more quickly than a life without a roof to call my own. So I told my mother that I was going to be making my own way in the world with or without her help. Iwalked, carrying Brooke and the few belongings I could stuff into a bag that hung from my shoulders to the YWCA, knowing it was a safe haven for many and that I would be the least abused of the women there, physically at least.

I bagged groceries at a locally-owned store, working long hours, picking Brooke up from the YWCA at the end of the day, crashing in the barracks provided for homeless women. Through it all, I remembered tosmile at customers, no matter how tired I was, and sometimes they would smile back. One man, with a smile brighter than the unchivalrous knights I had once associated with, bought groceries I would often see that evening in the food line at the shelter.

One evening, I slipped on a patch of ice, and he ran over to assist me, having just loaded bags of apples and oranges into his car. He lifted me to my feet and steadied my stance and asked if he could drive me to the shelter. The cold air and my ragged coat begged me to say yes. He walked me back to the car, offering his elbow for me to hold, and guided me to the passenger side, opened the door and ensured I was secure before he closed it again. We drove silently, my discomfort with compassion hitting a breaking point by the time we pulled into the parking lot of the shelter. He was parked and out of the car before my fingers found the handle of the door. He opened it, my hand now firmly on the handle, and I promptly fell out of the seat. He picked me up, again, and mutely begged forgiveness with his eyes for causing me any further embarrassment. He reached into the back seat, grabbed the two bags and walked in beside me.

He taught me to expect kindness and gracious smiles over a year of rides to the shelter.

He noticed the next winter that I had not bought myself a coat. Brooke had grown tremendously, and her needs exceeded mine. Before the second snowfall of the season, there was a heavy coat waiting on the passenger seat. He taught me to appreciate being cherished and protected.

When Brooke went to school for the first time, he made sure she had the backpack she wanted. He lifted her into the air to celebrate birthdays and first report cards. He taught Brooke to feel comfortable in another's arms. She ran to him after school to tell him everything that had happened, leaving me standing next to the car, arms outstretched but empty. It was an unexpectedly fulfilling emptiness.

He helped create a home I never wanted toescape, filling a corner of the small one-bedroom apartment we first shared with colourful books and prints from old nursery rhymes. He held her in his lap and let her turn the pages, spending time exploring thewords together. I watched them, happily and sadly, knowing I would never share in the experience.

He had started to teach me, but the words seemed to jump across the pages, and when I could get them to stand still, I had trouble comprehending anything beyond Dick and Jane's escapades.

Instead, I worked to repeat many of the words he used to try to provoke in me a higher interest. "Books are excellent in order to grow your mind and your heart. They open up your eyes to worlds you maynever have the chance to see. They teach you to respect other voices and teach you to listen carefully so that you understand the intent and the implications. Some are beautiful; some are sad. There are different kinds that are meant for different people, but each opens the same way and are accessible to all."

But I had never read one.

So, yes, I was incredibly jealous of my daughter's love affair with books, even if it meant that occasionally she'd read one that made her heart ache. This reaction seemed far more intense than I would have expected from the death of a main character, a dystopian society that can't be overcome, or the loss ofhope for the narrator based on either of these.

My mother had never granted me the time to deal with pain on my own, instead taxing me with chores and long stints of listening to biblical stories she put her own bent on, creating lethargy and an acceptance of the dullness in my life. I knew Brooke needed to learn to navigate the madness of fantasy, mystery, and classic novels, not to mention real life. And so I waited.

I stood at the bottom of the attic stairs that night. I listened to the muffled sounds, waiting to hear turning pages that echoed down the stairwell. Instead, I heard only exasperation and the tiniest sounds of discomfort I had ever heard. The next day, I waited for her to arrive for breakfast, leaving her eggs on the table until they solidified into a clump that slid off the plate into the trash can with little more than a poke from a fork. I waited for her to come down for lunch, fixing a sandwich that was eaten by the twins instead, when three o'clock chimed and they said they were hungry. I waited for her to specify a dinner request, and made macaroni and cheese, one she had said was a favorite, when I was running out of time. I waited at the foot of her stairs again, listening intently, grateful to hear only even breathing this time. The next morning, I cleared the bowl of macaroni and cheese, and I waited again.

Not patiently, but quietly.

Two days later, Brooke descended from the attic. Her eyes were sunken and she had lost a few precious pounds. She would not speak, but she held in her hands a book that did not look like any I had seen her carry before. Paperback, creased binding, corners of multiple pages turned down. It looked, to a casual observer, to be a well-loved book, though I knew better. Brooke cherished hardcovers, adored the extra heft associated with a solid binding. When she resigned herself to a paperback due to her limitedbudget, Brooke took precious care to not mark the book in any significant way. This book, though, seemed to have been taken through the chaos that I had only ever seen at our dinner table.

She placed the book on the counter, careful to miss the spots of water that were still there from cleaning the dishes that morning. She opened the refrigerator, despondency apparent in every movement. The girl who had never made a motion without strong and clear intent now stared into the appliance as though she could not remember what it was supposed to hold for her.

I offered Brooke everything I could think of to take away the vacantness behind her eyes. All were rejected, as Brooke claimed she wasn't hungry anyway, and she needed to write a paper. She shuffled back out of the kitchen, leaving the book on the counter. Father walked in, looked at it, looked at me, and said only, "Worst book ever. I can't believe they still make students read it."

While I had always been grateful for a roof, for the food, for the childhood free of bruises and broken arms, for the first time ever, I was grateful I had never learned to read if literacy meant misery.

I would never understand my daughter's love affair

with words; they never seemed safe after that. But I would respect the commitment she could make tothem even if I didn't understand why she wanted to experience the pain.

Jessie Blair

Jessie Blair is of Mohawk & Irish/Scottish ancestry. She attends the University of British Columbia, where she studies First Nations culture and history. She enjoys learning from the Elders and attends as many cultural events as she can. Her first short story is featured in a book entitled, *Anthology for a Green Planet* by Filidh Publishing. "Fundamental Challenges" is her second published short story. She lives with her husband in Vancouver, British Columbia.

Fundamental Challenges

My girlfriend is beautiful and even more tempting when her lips puckered to blow out the last candle on the table before we went to bed. Our eyes met as the smoke passed her face. Her eyes lit up as though they had taken the flame from the candle. She licked her lips and smiled at me, leaving me breathless, helpless to her charms. Jaki, that was her name, slipped the black lace camisole from her shoulders, my eyes hungrily following her camisole to the floor. I stared at the lingerie next to her ankles, afraid to look up at what I already knew was the most beautiful woman I'd ever seen. "Christina, is something wrong?" she asked me seductively. I answered no but still didn't look up at her. Finally, my eyes lifted from the camisole that lay on the floor, following every curve of her body until our eyes met. Having been brought up in a white conservative Christian home, I never thought I would ever fall in love with a black *man,* let alone a black woman. But this felt right.

"I love you, Jaki." The words rushed out of my mouth like wild water rushing out of a broken dam. I leapt up from my chair, eagerly embraced her, andkissed her passionately. "I love you too, Chris," Jaki whispered in my ear.

I really never thought our relationship would come to this point. We first met in a *Sociology of Religion* class at University. I was doing my usual "smart-ass-talk-like-I-know-it-all" routine. After all, I was one of the few born-again Christians in this class; who better to know about religion than I?

This memory is so clear, as though it were yesterday. We were in class and discussing our thoughts about religion. As though on cue, as a credit to my faith, or so I thought, I stood up and proclaimed that Christianity was the only true religion because the Bible stated that Jesus was the only Saviour of mankind, and the Bible itself is true. My proclamation was interrupted by an assertive female voice from the back saying something to the effect that "the Bible has been tampered with by bishops and popes for centuries in order to reflect the doctrines of the Christian church at the time, and especially to subjugate women."

I was astounded by these shocking words and wondered who had said them. I jerked my head around to find my eyes fall upon the prettiest girl in the class. She had rich, deep mocha-coloured skin and a voluptuous figure. Her long black hair was corn-rowed, and it framed her soft, round face, accentuating the largest, softest, brownest eyes I had ever seen. Pursing her lips and glaring at me, she added, "Christianity has been stealing doctrines from the pagan religions from day one: Christmas, Easter, Valentine's Day, the trinity..."

As she continued her list of doctrines, I was searching for an exit from the room with my eyes. Not only did I feel humiliated, I felt hated. I thought this woman should not be questioning the Bible and Christianity. My pale white skin had turned a bright crimson red from the rush of emotions that I was experiencing. Gulping, I took my seat quietly and began to realize that she was, indeed, entitled to her own opinion even if I knew she was wrong. At the end of the class, as I was putting my books in my bag, when she approached me, apologized and hoped there were no hard feelings. "Religion is a very touchy subject with me," she said.

"I'm Jaki" she smiled and shook my hand.

Returning the smile, I introduced myself, "Chris is what my friends call me."

"Let's get some lunch."

"Sure," I replied, thinking this would be a good chance to set a proper Christian example. When we arrived at the cafeteria, there was a bit of a lineup for lunch, so we talked.

"You seem to not like Christianity" I said.

"I don't have anything against Christianity per se; I just don't like evangelical Christians."

Taken aback by that statement, I asked, "Why? They only preach that Jesus loves everyone."

"They say dogmatically that Jesus loves everyone who is Christian."

"Don't you believe that Jesus died for our sins?"

"I believe that Jesus died because of the sins of the religious leaders of his time. They were jealous of Jesus and his power."

"Of course, his power came from God."

"So you say."

"Where else could it come from?" I could hear the terse tone in my voice.

"Jesus was a magician."

I laughed at Jaki's statement. "Tell me you don't honestly believe that."

"Well, no, I don't. But if you really think about it, it's no more far-fetched an idea than Jesus being everybody's saviour." Our eyes locked intensely, and my jaw stiffened with tension. She continued: "Why do Christians insist that theirs is the true religion when most of their doctrines are pagan?"

I was getting pretty upset by now. Suddenly I blurted out, "I'm sorry, I can't have lunch with you today. Jesus said that the world would not understand him." I left the cafeteria feeling angrier than ever. "What nerve!" I thought. "I'm going to prove her wrong!"

Filled with determination, I went to the library and began reading information on Christian history and doctrines. I was not at the library even an hour when I came across an encyclopedia article about the origins of Christmas. I could not believe what I was reading.

I was confused, so I went to talk to Reverend Kerr. Reverend Kerr was middle-aged, and he had known me almost my whole life. He had a way of making life seem better.

I sat down beside him in the church pew and asked him, "Why do Christians keep Christmas if it's a pagan holiday?"

Rev. Kerr answered, "I am aware that Christmas has pagan origins, but we keep it to honour Christ."

"How do we know it actually honours Christ and doesn't insult Him?"

Reverend Kerr gave me a knowing smile, "I remember struggling with this concept when I was in university too. The Lord understands our intentions. He understands that we celebrate Christmas and Easter to honour Him."

I stared wide-eyed at him as the thoughts spun around my mind. "If we keep pagan holidays as Christian holidays, then how can we sit in judgment of those who are not Christian?"

"As you know, the Bible states that no man can come to God except through Jesus. We do not judge people. We are concerned about their salvation. Chris, out of curiosity, what has happened to make you question your faith?"

"A girl in my *Sociology of Religion* class told me that Christianity borrowed many of its doctrines from paganism. I got angry at her and set out to prove her wrong only to find out she was right."

"The Devil throws a lot of confusion and temptation in the path of those who are following Jesus. It sounds as though this is a trick that he is playing on you. Pray for guidance and wisdom, and get support from other Christians. There's a Bible Study tonight I would strongly urge you to attend".

I was in a confused haze. I thought perhaps he was right about needing to be closer to other people in the faith, so I told him I would be at Bible Study.

At Bible Study that evening, I felt comfortable because I was back among people of like mind. I listened intently to what Rev. Kerr had to say. After the main message, the minister broke everyone into smaller discussion groups. I ended up being in a group with two visitors from New York City. A younger man named James and his Grandmother, Rosa. James had a slim build and striking dark hair. He also had the gift of gab. He just wouldn't be quiet, and after a while, his non-stop talking got on my nerves.

James asked everybody in the group, "What's your favourite scripture?" Everybody took a turn to answer his question, and finally, it was my turn.

I was so annoyed at this point that I said, "Even a fool when he is silent, people will think he is wise."

James gasped, "What do you mean by that?"

I shrugged my shoulders and played innocent, "That's my favourite scripture."

James was not satisfied. He looked around the group and repeated the question in a louder voice, "What does she mean by that?"

Rosa was becoming exasperated with James and said to him in a New York Italian accent, "She doesn't mean anything by it. You asked a question; she's answerin' ya."

James rolled his eyes at his Grandmother and sighed.

"Don't roll your eyes at me!" his Grandmother snapped. James let the subject go and was actually quiet for a few minutes.

I left Bible Study that night feeling smug about my comment to James, and I felt good about my belief system.

***

The next week I was in class and overheard Jaki talking to somebody else. I turned around and looked in her direction until she looked back. Jaki excused herself from the conversation and came over to me. "Chris, I'm sorry that I upset you the other day. May I buy you lunch?"

I smiled and said, "OK."

Over lunch, Jaki told me she had been doing a lot of thinking on the subject of Christian and pagan doctrine. "I shouldn't have pushed so hard to make my point," she said apologetically.

I replied, "After our discussion, I went to the library and found out that what you said about Christmas was correct. It was a pagan holiday."

She was surprised and impressed by my actions.

"What are your conclusions?"

"I spoke with my pastor, and he explained that Christians keep Christmas as a way to honour Christ."

Jaki smiled and said, "I'm glad you have found peace with your faith again."

I enthusiastically continued talking, "Yeah, it's really important that pagans be shown how to live God's way."

Jaki looked down at the table and sighed, "Perhaps some pagans already know how to be in tune with God."

I snarked, "A person can't know God unless they acknowledge Jesus as their personal saviour."

Jaki calmly replied, "There are many types of spiritual paths, and all of them have value."

"There are many types of spirituality, but the only true way is through Jesus."

"I don't want to argue about this, Chris."

"Salvation comes through Jesus. I am worried about your soul Jaki, because without Jesus in your life, you will perish."

At this point, Jaki had heard enough.

She looked at me and said, "I need to leave shortly, but before I go, I want to say this to you. If we're going to be friends, I need you to respect that my beliefs are different from yours. So, when I hear you say that my soul will perish because my beliefs are different from yours, I feel insulted because I don't believe your spirituality makes you a better person than I am. People are not objects to be converted."

Jaki got up to leave.

"I'm sorry you feel that way."

"I'm sorry you feel so strongly about your religion that you're allowing it to get in the way of our friendship."

Jaki then left, and I was in a quandary about our friendship.

"How can I save Jaki?" I thought to myself.

***

It was Wednesday, and I caught the bus to go to the Seniors' Social Tea at the church. I wasn't even on the bus for five minutes when much to my surprise Jaki got on.

Our eyes met; Jaki smiled and came over to talk. I felt an anxious tightness in my stomach.

"Hi Chris!" said Jaki with a big smile

"Hi Jaki," I replied nervously.

"I haven't heard from you for a few days. How are you?"

"I've been busy. I'm okay. How are you?"

"I'm on my way to the Royal Ontario Museum. They have some new objects in the Egyptian wing."

As Jaki continued speaking about the museum, I had a vision of us passionately kissing each other. I felt a sharp, stinging pain run down my spine like a lightning bolt hitting my body. I was in shock at the thought that I was attracted to another woman. These feelings were new to me, and I wanted to hide them; I wanted to delete those feelings. I thought to myself that a true Christian woman does not experience same-sex attraction.

Just then, I came back to reality. Jaki was saying goodbye because she was at her stop. I sheepishly returned her goodbye.

I could not keep my mind in the present moment even after Jaki left. I kept dwelling on that imaginary and passionate kiss with Jaki. I started praying that God would help me fight this – whatever this was- becauseI wasn't convinced that I *had* romantic feelings for Jaki. But the image kept wandering back into my mind. I struggled and struggled, but it wouldn't go away. I was alarmed when the older lady in the seat behind me said, "that asthma of yours sounds bad. Maybe you should open up the window?"

I gave her a puzzled look and asked, "Am I breathing heavily?"

"Yes, do you have a puffer for your Asthma?"

I gently told her I didn't have Asthma, and the woman gave me a concerned look.

"Maybe you should get checked by your doctor."

I thanked her for that suggestion, then opened the window and lowered my head to my chest. The cool breeze felt refreshing against the warm skin of my neck. There was a single thought on my mind at that moment. How would I, as a Christian woman, deal with my attraction to Jaki?

When I got to the church, I saw Reverend Kerr and went to talk to him.

"You look worried, Chris. What's happening?"

"I'm not sure. I just had a very strange vision of me kissing another woman."

Rev. Kerr's mouth hung open slightly as he stared at me. He then shook his head for a second and snapped out of his shock.

"Keep praying. Stay close to God. I will keep you in my prayers too." He looked at me in a very concerned and fatherly way and then patted my shoulder reassuringly. We smiled at each other as though trying to tell ourselves this would solve my problem. Of course, it didn't.

The next few months were a hellish nightmare. I would pray continuously that God would give me the strength, courage and conviction to fight my weakness for Jaki. I spoke several times to Reverend Kerr, and we prayed together to give me strength. Yet, every time I had contact with Jaki, those romantic feelings came back and seemed to be growing stronger. One day I decided to tell Jaki about my attraction to her in the hopes that she would be appalled. It was my hope that Jaki would end the friendship so that I did not have to agonize over my spiritual life hanging in the balance because of my growing attraction to her. Much to my surprise, Jaki was rather receptive to the idea of discussing my attraction to her. I tried to impress upon Jaki that my attraction to her would mean the end of my Christian spiritual path.

Jaki inquired how it would be the end of my life as a Christian; after all, there are several Gay-positive churches I could attend.

I didn't foresee that answer at all, and it caught me off guard, but it was a comfort to realize that I had options. I could have both my sexual identity and my spiritual life. I didn't have to choose.

I started smiling widely as that comforting concept rested within my heart and soul as though it was waiting for a place of rest. A sigh of relief escaped through my lips, releasing all the worry and tension that had been building up inside me until I remembered all the praying I had been doing for strength and guidance to fight my attraction to Jaki. My thoughts began to race at that moment between comforting thoughts and feelings of dread. Comforting thoughts such as, "All my prayers the past few months have solidified my romantic feelings rather than vanquish them," to the dreadful thought that, "I am going to go to hell because homosexuality is against God's teachings."

The anxiety building up inside me at the thought that I was going to go to hell burst forth from within me in uncontrollable tears and sobbing. Jaki brought her chair around to my side of the table to sit beside me and put her arm around my shoulders.

"I'm here for you." I put my head on her shoulder and told her about my fear of going to hell.

"You're not going to hell. Not every Christian church believes that homosexuals are going to hell."

Once again, my whole body heaved a sigh of relief, and I stopped crying, although my chin was still quivering. It was at this precise moment that Jaki and I had our first kiss, a kiss that changed my world. Our lips met softly. We savoured every moment and talked for a long time after. During our conversation, I decided to stop going to my current church and try a Gay-positive church instead. I was very anxious about embarking upon this new life, and I expressed concern to Jaki about what I would tell Reverend Kerr about my decision.

"Tell him that you no longer share his beliefs and leave it at that," suggested Jaki. I liked her answer because it was short, sweet and to the point.

Jaki had given me a fresh outlook on life. My life had totally changed, and for the better. I could finally accept myself and my sexual identity. I had a big smile on my face for the next few days. My passion for Jaki was getting the better of me, so I mustered up the nerve to invite her over for dinner at my apartment. I lit soft white candles all over the apartment, put on a low-cut red dress and an Ella Fitzgerald CD. I popped the fireplace video into the DVD player just for extra ambience. In the middle of the table was one red rose to symbolize true love and a white candle beside it to symbolize purity because I truly loved her. Then it came, the knock on the door: each knock a beat of my heart. I tried to restrain myself as I approached the door. Then taking a big breath, I opened it to see Jaki in a beautiful black dress suit. We greeted each other with a kiss, and I asked her in.

"Make yourself comfortable on the couch." I said,

"I brought some wine for us," she replied.

I reached my hand into the brown bag and pulled out a bottle of Chardonnay. "Oh! My favourite! Thank you!" I leaned in to steal a kiss.

When I leaned back from the kiss, I noticed just how breathtakingly beautiful she was. I also noted her cleavage showing, which is, of course, where my eyes rested.

"If you're finished staring at my chest, maybe you can tell me what we're having for dinner," she said, smiling at me.

I was embarrassed and mumbled, "Sorry, just enjoying the beautiful view." Then I quickly recovered from the embarrassment and asked, jokingly, if I could have her for dessert. We looked longingly into each other's eyes, all the while smiling.

"God! I hope you *do* have me for dessert!"

We then fell into each other's arms in a passionate embrace and began French kissing. Our bodies were hungry for each other. Our hands were eagerly groping each other's bodies. "Oh God," I thought, "This is it! The moment I had waited for so very anxiously. I really want to do this." I ran my hand over her clothed breast. She was gorgeous, and I loved her because she had such a different perspective on life.

Just then, the smoke alarm started going off. The loud beeping noise filled the apartment and startled both of us. When we realized what it was, we both started laughing, touched our foreheads together, and kissed briefly.

"Dinner's ready!" We both laughed, and she quipped, "That puts a whole new meaning to the phrase 'ring the dinner bell'!" Our laughter turned to guffaws. I made my way to the kitchen, and she started opening all the windows to let the smoke out. I was busy tending to the burnt roast when I heard her seductively say,

"Baby, it may be cold outside, but it sure is hot in here!"

I whipped my head around to see her smiling and wearing only a lacy black camisole. My body tingled with anticipation. I felt my heart pounding, and my hands were sweaty. In my dreams of this moment, I was so very confident, and instead, I felt so very inadequate. Then the moment came when she was completely naked, there was no containing myself. The words "I love you" fell from my lips. I eagerly embraced her, and we made love.

We have been together ever since. There are no regrets. Jaki is my true love and companion.

Katie Horricks-King

Katie Horricks-King comes from a family of literary adepts. Writing seriously since she was 15, she dabbled when she was younger but lost the bug. Now working on five novels, she's balancing (or trying to) a toddler, her dad, painting, a cat, and being nuttier than a fruitcake. She can sometimes be spotted, if you're looking carefully, dancing through the forests of Vancouver Island.

First Born

I can feel it coming. It's only a matter of time now. Death is stalking me with his pale horse. I know I'll come back, that this is only my human death, but I still fear it. I fear the pain of the Change. I fear losing my connection to my baby sister. We already lost our mom four months ago today – I don't know how she'll handle me once this is done. I can feel himcoming – he's almost here!

I woke with a start. An erratic sound clamoured for my attention. It took me a moment to realize that I had fallen asleep by Amelia's hospital bed, and a moment more to realize that my phone was ringing.

"'Ello," I answered it with a well-practiced flick of my wrist. I stifled a yawn as my fiancé's voice came through the tiny speaker.

"Serenity, how are you darling? How's your sister?" His tone held genuine concern. He didn't know what I was, what we were. He was human, and I told him Amelia had been hit by a car, instead of beaten to the brink of death.

"She's stable. Doctor's confident he can bring her out of the coma by the beginning of next week," I straightened in my uncomfortable chair.

"That's great news! You sound exhausted, though. Did you fall asleep in that chair again? Why don't you come home and rest? I'll make you something to eat, then we can curl up for a few hours, and you can return to your watch post."

That was Kevin. Always cheerful and looking after others.

I nodded, then realized he couldn't see it. "I'll be home as soon as I remind the nurses to call me if there are any changes. Food sounds wonderful."

"Homemade waffles?" his voice was infectious in its joy.

"With whipped cream?" I smiled.

"And fresh plum jam," he gave a low chuckle.

"See you soon."

"I love you."

"I love you too." Even though I lie to you every day about who and what I am. We hung up, and I wentto find a nurse. One happened to be at the desk in the ICU, but she waved me off before I could approach.

"I know, Serenity. Call you if there's even the slightest blip. We've got her, don't worry," Barbara-Anne flashed me a small smile.

"Thank you," I inclined my head to her and made my way to the stairs. They were faster than the elevator and got me a smidgeon of exercise.

The parking lot was quiet, and I beeped my car open. Falling into the warm bucket seat, I closed my eyes as I turned the key, almost hoping it wouldn't start so I could stay with my only remaining family. It clicked over easily, and I sighed, opening my eyes to the late-fall sun. The drive home was quiet, and as I pulled up the driveway, I could see a number of lights on.

Getting out, I inhaled deeply and smiled. Fresh, homemade waffles like my mother used to make teased my nose as I pulled open the kitchen door, but I frowned upon entering. Kevin wasn't there. Tired, I took my coat off and hung it on the back of a chair. My shoes followed, and I made my way through the pale peach living room and up the stairs. Sounds I wasn't expecting led me to the bedroom Kevin and I shared, and the first thing I saw on pushing the door open was a pair of massive fake breasts.

The blonde attached to the stiff globes gave a scream of pleasure as Kevin thrust against her skinny ass. Shock held me in place as he looked up and smiled.

"Hey, babe. I wasn't expecting you back quite so soon," he was barely winded.

I turned and ran. I was down the stairs and out the door without a single glance back. I ran to the only place I could think of; the small cliff over a small phosphorescent lake. I tripped over a rock near the top and didn't get up again. My heart was shredding. Humans were cruel, evil.

It wasn't long before footsteps crunched the dying grass behind me. I looked up, then scrambled to my feet. Kevin stood there in sweatpants, skate shoes and a light hoodie. He smiled.

"You weren't supposed to see that, babe. Unlike that whore, you were supposed to be my love." He was weirdly calm. There was no emotion at all in his eyes.

"And you're a pervert!" I threw at him. How had I missed the psychopath hiding in his skin? How had I not seen that he wasn't a great guy?

He laughed at that. "No, Serenity. But you, unfortunately, have to die. You were supposed to be my perfect trophy, but that can't happen now." His arm came out from behind him, a gun in his hand. He raised it. "I wish things had been different."

He pulled the trigger. I remember a flash, the BANG!, and a quick, explosive pain in my forehead. The pain vanished, and I could feel myself falling but couldn't stop it. Why couldn't I blink? I felt my body hit the ground, but it didn't hurt. Kevin walked away, laughing, not looking back.

The sun sank, and as the last rays fell behind the mountains, I felt it start—The Change. The bullet exited the hole it created, and the tissue knit shut behind it. My eyes burned for a long moment, changing, becoming predator eyes. A scream was torn from my lips as my bones seemed to break and reform all at once. When it was done, the moon was bright in the sky, and I thirsted for vengeance. Instinct was my ruler, and no one could stand in my way.

What felt like only moments later, I came back to myself. I was sitting in my car, back in the hospital parking lot. I glanced at the rear-view mirror and grimaced at the blood caked on my forehead. I tried rubbing it off, but it wouldn't budge. Sighing, I pulled the hood of my sweater over my head and as low as it would go. Pocketing my keys, I exited the car and made my way to the elevator, too tired for the stairs this time.

The doors opened, and three people stepped out as I was reaching for the button. Stepping inside, I hit the required button and leaned against the wall. Thankfully, no one else seemed to need this particular lift. I kept my head low when I reached the ICU. Nurses had a way of overreacting when blood was involved. Mary had taken over for Barbara-Anne while I was gone, and the aged redhead smiled at me. I nodded back and slipped into my sister's room. She hadn't moved.

Taking my usual seat, I slid my hand under Amelia's and gripped her fingers. The bruises on her face were just yellow tinges now, a little darker in some spots, but healing. I laid my head on the bed and lost myself in the sound of her steady breathing.

A gentle touch on my shoulder startled me some time later. Doctor Trenton, or Doctor Yummy as I called him in my head, smiled. Then frowned and touched my forehead.

"What the hell happened, Serenity?" his voice was low and melodic.

"You remember the story I told you of the first-born sisters in my family?"

"Of course. The elder dies within six months of their mother and is changed so she can protect her sister until the youngest daughter of the younger sister turns fourteen."

"I died today. I am no longer a being of creation; I am an agent of destruction with a single purpose."

"Let's get you cleaned up. My shift just ended, and Amelia is stable. You'll probably need to hunt, too," he sidestepped my statement with apparent ease. His being a vampire helped. He was around five and a half thousand years old. Give or take a couple of decades.

I sighed and stood, looking at him briefly before going to the door. He had a hand on it before I could touch the handle.

"Have you seen your eyes?"

"No. Why?"

"They're red and gold, not green and gold."

I frowned. "How are we going to explain that?"

"I'll think of something. But, you still need to feed."

"I know. I'm not sure if I want to, though."

"Then feed on me. We both know that vampires can feed off each other in times where food is scarce."

"It's about the emotion in the blood, not the blood itself," I nodded.

"Let me take you home, get you cleaned up, then fed."

I sighed. I shouldn't be doing this. I wanted to, had felt the pull of him since we met, but going with him would probably destroy the last of my sanity. If I even had any left.

"She'll be okay?" I finally asked.

"She will. The infection is gone, and the swelling around her brain is no longer dangerous. We can come right back after if you want to."

"Thanks," I let him open the door and follow me out.

"My pleasure," he whispered in my ear as I passed him. It sent a shiver down my spine.

Our venture to his car was quick and silent. The drive back to his apartment was equally so, except for the purr of his engine. He didn't feel the need to break the silence until we stood outside his penthouse suite, and he was entering the unlock code. We stepped inside and he entered a second set of numbers into the little box on the wall.

"I apologize for the mess. I wasn't expecting to have anyone over when I left earlier."

"It's quite all right," I shrugged. "I wasn't expecting to go anywhere but home earlier."

"Touché. Bathroom is the door on your left there. Fresh towels are on the rack beside the shower."

"Thanks."

"My pleasure," he inclined his head.

Taking my shoes off, I opened the bathroom door and barely paid any attention to the bright room as I stripped off. My clothes hit the floor, leaving a trail to the frosted shower stall. It was roomy, and the water was hot when I finally figured out how to get it working.

I probably stayed in longer than I should have, but I had a Lady Macbeth moment when I found some dried blood underneath one of my fingernails. It didn't last long, but it reminded me to double-scrub the area around where the bullet had entered my skull.

I dawdled as long as I could. I knew I had to, but I really didn't want to feed. I wasn't a true vampire, not by a long shot, but feeding kept me sane. If I ever run across my father again, I'll be sure to thank his half-breed ass.

Pushing a button on the wall, the water shut off, and I got out, grabbing a thick, fluffy towel on my way by. I used it on my hair first, then wrapped it around my body before exiting the bathroom and following the lights to the kitchen.

James had shucked his shirt and stood over the stove in nothing but a pair of very snug jeans. Bacon sizzled, and my mouth watered, both at the sight of his well-muscled back and the cooking food.

"Take a seat; it will be ready in a moment," he said without looking away from what he was doing.

I pulled a stool out from the island and sat. Watching his muscles ripple at the slightest movement triggered something in me, and I felt my fangs extend. I studied him, searched for a pulse but didn't find one.

"I will not make my heart beat until after you have some real food, Serenity," James glanced back at me. "This part of you will be harder to control now. It will be more tied to your base emotions than it was before."

"How do you know that?" my voice held an odd bass note.

"The same thing happens when half-bloods are bitten and turned completely. Their human half acted as a buffer between them and the hunger; when the buffer was gone, they had to learn everything all over again."

I shook my head, trying to clear it of the fog. "How long will it take to relearn control?"

"I don't know," he set a plate of bacon and eggs in front of me. "It's different for everyone."

I sighed and picked up a piece of crispy bacon. My fangs retracted, and I scarfed down the food in silence. As soon as I was done, the plate vanished, and James took my hands. A slow, steady pulse beat under his pale flesh as he led me to the living room and sat, pulling me into his lap as he tilted his head to stretch his neck.

"Feast, Serenity. Taking too much won't kill me."

I looked into his blazing blue eyes for only a moment before I bit into his throat. Blood gushed into my mouth, and I drank it greedily; the warmth, happiness and love –

I snapped back and jumped away from him. He sat there with a look on his face that was half supreme ecstasy and half confusion. He reached out to me as his face shifted to pleading.

"Please, Serenity. Don't stop," he moaned. "Let me love you."

I stared at him, dumbstruck.

"There are no secrets between us, no lies," he continued. "You'll never have to pretend around me."

I wanted it. I really did. Love without lies. It was an alien concept to me. Except for Amelia and our mom, I had always had to hide, and familial love was different than romantic. I had never had the satisfaction of true romantic love.

"Okay," I nodded, slipping back into his lap and returning to his throat. "Okay."

Karma

Year: 482 million BCE. Language adjusted to current human for comprehension.

Hello. My name is Eros. Yes, that Eros. God of Love, Son of Aphrodite, yadda, yadda, yadda. Since you probably already have an idea of my base purpose, my *raison d'être*, let's clear some things up.

First: I'm not a little cherub in diapers who goes around SHOOTING people. Sheeze, I'm not violent. Unless you threaten me or mine – then I'll just kill you.

Second: my height does not change. I am 6 feet, 3 inches tall. I enjoy being tall. It lets me look down at women's clothing while they think I'm looking at their faces.

Third: I am very particular about how I keep my hair. Since I can change my appearance at will, I like to keep my hair as my signature thing. As such, I make sure it always looks like a domino, all black and white chunks. My eyes are also this really weird chartreuse green—no idea why, and I can't change them.

Fourth: I control your brain. Finito. End of story. Oh, you want me to explain that? Okay. I take one look at your thoughts, your past and your future and flip a switch in your brain that releases chemicals. These chemicals dictate your actions, your feelings. They can change your thoughts. One minute you could be buying slaves to abuse, and the next – becauseslavers, abusers, liars and rapists, to name a few, really piss me off – the next you're fucking a goat out in someone's field because you're madly in love with it. Not that I would actually do that to the poor goat.

Anyway, you're probably wondering why I'm talking to you. Truth be told, I don't really know. I guess I just need to tell someone how I fell in love. Yeah, me. Who knew it would hurt so much to be hit by your own specialty.

Her name was Psyche Eleni Argyros, and she was perfection. She was part of the experimental race the other gods and I had created as a parallel to thisplanet's natural species. We had wanted to see how a more advanced, more evolved version of humans would grow and develop in our city. Atlantis the Beautiful.

Some were kind. Some were not. Eventually, one tribe of women wound up ruling everyone, and they enslaved men. Used them as breeders and work horses. The city flourished, and they built us temples to thank us for their creation.

After a few thousand years, I got bored. Seriously, it's really easy when you're already a couple hundred million years old. So, I wandered. Through the city, in and around until I caught the faintest whiff of jasmine, well, more like its ancestral plant, but you get the idea. It piqued my interest. Temple Row and the main palace were the only places with flowers within the city walls; the rest was agricultural space. I followed the faint hints as they wafted to me until I reached my mother's temple. All Mother love that woman; she always had the most nubile of priestesses. Surprisingly, most of them virgins. Kind of weird for the goddess who was/is the embodiment of human and animal fertility.

It was there that I first saw her. She was in a sheer light green dress that both hid her from prying eyes and left nothing to my rather perverted imagination. She was standing by the fountain behind the altar, and little white flowers seemed to float in her knee-length, coppery-brown hair. I must have made a sound, Idon't know, but she startled and stared at me in alarm; her perfectly blended dark chocolate and new grass- green eyes wide and bright.

She opened her mouth – and what a mouth it was! – with a scream teetering on the tip of her tongue. I snapped my fingers and stole her voice because screaming is loud and annoying, and it would summon my mother, who would take me over her knee with a flogger. Aphrodite is one scary woman if you piss her off. She's almost as bad as Tisiphone, or her daughter Rylynne. Sheeze, those two take it to a whole new level.

Anyways, back to Psyche the Luminous. She threw a bowl at me. A fucking antique bowl. Right at my head. She had good aim, and it clocked me in the temple. Normally, it wouldn't have fazed me, but the novelty of it had me keeling over. She did that gorgeous gasp of concern that so many women have trouble perfecting and rushed over, fussing over it and

giving me the perfect view down her dress. Up close, she was at least six feet tall – abnormally tall compared to everyone else in the city. Since she wasn't looking and was no longer in danger of screaming, I gave her back her voice and instantly
regretted it. It was soft, melodic, and gave me the most painful hard-on I have ever had.

"You were supposed to duck and run, you idiot!" she didn't yell, but I could feel her force of will pressing at me.

I groaned. Her voice was honeyed torture. "I was following the faint traces of jasmine," I rubbed my head.

"Men are not supposed to enter here without their owners. Where is yours? Why is she not with you?"

"I have no owner."

"Impossible! All men in this city are owned by someone."

"With exceptions," I winked at her; I couldn't help it.

"There are no exceptions!" she was getting angry with me, her face flushing a little as her eyes brightened.

My mother chose that moment to pop out of wherever she was. "Eros, what have you done to anger my high priestess?"

"I followed the flowers in her hair and startled her," I grinned as she jumped away and rubbed her hands on her dress.

Aphrodite shook her head at me. "What have I told you about scaring my girls?"

"Don't do it, or you'll spank me," I sighed. "Does it matter that I didn't mean to this time?"

"Did she hit you with anything?"

"The bowl I got you for your birthday seven hundred years ago."

"Did it actually hurt?"

"Yes..."

"Then I won't paddle your ass. Just don't do it again. Psyche, me dear, come with me. We must talk," she pulled the beautiful human away as I lay there. They disappeared into the inner halls of the temple as I froze the image of her distinctive eyes in my mind. The deep dark brown and brilliant green were completely separate colours and practically glowed with her anger. By their colour alone, I knew she was at least a couple of generations away from a Creator – beings of immense power who serve the
All Mother, who is herself the original Creator and a remnant of the last universe.

I shook my head, and waves of coppery-brown hair

surrounded the eyes in my mind. Mother knew. She had to. That woman was torture for me. Getting to my feet, I thought about following them but realized retreat might salvage a little bit of my ego. Not that I actually had much left after letting a bowl hit me. I was about to teleport, for lack of a better term, back to my temple when Rylynne,
Goddess of Time, Blood, Battle and Sunshine, pulled me into her haven in limbo.

"Dude, you're an idiot," she laughed at me, her tangerine eyes bright with mirth.

"Mind telling me what you already know will happen?" I couldn't help but smile back. I could never frown when she was happy, no matter how hard I tried.

"Start at the beginning, or the part you won't like?"

"Beginning."

"Her great-great-great-great-great-grandmother was one of the All Mother's soul keepers."

"Was?" This time I did manage a frown.

"She had to be reabsorbed after a vampire went nuts and attacked her."

"Shit."

"Indeed."

"What's the part I won't like?"

Rylynne grinned. "She's immune to you. Your abilities related to emotional control will never work on her."

"FUCK!" I couldn't stop the expletive from bursting out.

Her grin widened. "That's not even the worst of it."

I didn't want to hear this. I really didn't. However, morbid curiosity made me stay and listen.

"What's the worst?"

"You marry her."

I sat down. I couldn't help it. Me? Married? It wasn't something I had ever thought about. Or wanted to. Sure, I had fun getting humans to do it – but me?

"Does Mother know?" I finally managed to ask.

"'Dite? Of course, she does. She knew before Psyche was born."

"Did you tell her?"

"No. Like my mother, she knows things that will affect us long into a future that even I cannot see," Rylynne shook her head, setting her blood-red curls bouncing.

I thought about it for a minute. Or ten. "Will we be happy? I mean, will she love me?"

She popped one of her nifty windows open. Images came to life, and a woman in weird clothes that I had never seen before began to speak.

"Today, we will be studying the myths surrounding Eros and Psyche. According to the texts that have survived, their love was, for lack of a better term, epic. What happened varies between the times the texts were written and the translations, but the accepted story is that Psyche was a princess whose father refused to marry her to someone he did not think was worthy. Eventually, word reached Aphrodite that a human was being worshiped for her beauty rather than the goddess. Her anger was great, so she sent her son, Eros, to strike her with one of his golden arrows while in the markets. However, Eros fell in love with her himself. He sent word to the king through the Oracle of Delphi that the gods required her for a sacrifice and that she was to be dressed in her finest then left at the cliffs. The king did it, tearfully, and Eros stole her away to one of his temples later that night..."

The image faded away, the window closing behind it. Rylynne smiled at me.

"Does that answer your question?"

"Yes and no."

"It'll take you a while to wrap your head around it."

"Thanks for letting me know."

"You can't fight it, so don't try. Jasmine is her favourite flower, and amethysts do amazing things to her eyes."

"How do you know me so well?" I sighed, standing slowly.

"I'm older than you," she shrugged. "I watched you grow up, and you're the only other natural-born power on this planet. You know as well as I do that we have a bond the others don't understand. It's how I know that she will be your soul, your guiding light through the darkest of times."

I arched an eyebrow at her. "Is something badgoing to happen, Ry? You don't normally share this much."

She was silent for a moment, then a voice I really didn't like spoke. "Darkness is coming. There is still time to prepare. Hold tight to those you cherish, for they will be your only salvation." She shook her head again and cleared her throat. The bassy growl the words had come with always hurt her.

"Any idea what that means?"

"Not a damned clue. It will become clear in time, though. It always does." She got up slowly and stretched her neck. "You should get back before Aphrodite changes her mind about your future andkills her most loyal high priestess."

"Thanks, babe," I flashed her a grin before popping

back to my temple. Or, more accurately, Rylynne dropped me on my ass in the main bedroom. Sometimes, I really couldn't shake the feeling that she didn't like me. Nah, not possible. Everyone loves me.

Now, I could spell out the rest of our actual history, but I'm late for a ceremony, and you already know the gist of it. I got her to fall in love with me, we got married, and Persephone stopped the calendar on her life. It's been almost half a billion years, and we're still going strong. To quote some random drunk dude, Love cannot live without his Soul.

Mm, and if you want to read my detailed history, you'll just have to wait for me to free up some time to dictate it to this human I'm using as my personal assistant. Ciao for now -*Eros*

Kelly Duff

Kelly Duff lives in Victoria, BC. She has loved reading and writing since she was a little girl. "S.M.A." is her first short story publication.

S.M.A.

Going to Social Media Anonymous or S.M.A. every Tuesday evening used to be something Todd dreaded with every fibre of his being. He didn't want to hear about other people's problems living in the 'real world.' He could function there just fine if he wanted to. He just didn't see a point. Why should he? Online he only had to talk to people he wanted to talk to, who had similar interests. Through online gaming, he made friends with people from all over the world. Offline, Todd was incredibly shy and often found it hard to make friends. He was content with his online commitments. His mother, however, was not. Todd had promised her that he would at least try S.M.A. So every Tuesday, he spent an uneventful hour and a half in the meeting.

Then he met Jane. Beautiful Jane. She was smart, sweet, kind and best of all she understood him! She didn't think it was strange or abnormal that he had 453 followers on Twitter that he kept up a regular correspondence with. She admired his dedication. He admired hers as well. Jane had 762 friends on Facebook, all of whom she could remember intimate details about. At first, he wasn't sure that they would be compatible, as they didn't agree on social media platforms. They soon discovered, however, that they both belonged to a local chat group. And so their relationship began.

At first, they just talked about S.M.A. and their individual progress with the program. They discovered that they had both joined the program because their families were worried about them. Todd's mother had become incredibly upset and insisted he seek counselling after he had gone three weeks without going outside. Jane's sister had organized a family intervention for Jane after the fourth time Jane had nearly been hit by a car while updating her Facebook status.

As they continued to chat, Jane and Todd discovered they had a lot of similar interests. Todd felt like they had a real connection. They talked about everything, and he soon found that he felt comfortable telling Jane things he had never told anyone. When he told her how he felt, she agreed that she, too, felt she could tell him anything. Todd was really excited about the possibility of having an offline or IRL (in real life) relationship with Jane. If they could get there. They'd been chatting nearly nightly for about two months, but when they saw each other at the weekly meetings, they couldn't seem to hold a proper conversation. So far, the most they had been able to do is awkwardly smile, say a quick hi and then sit down, usually at opposite sides of the room. It was very frustrating for Todd! He really wanted to get to know Jane offline. He had never wanted that with anyone else. It both excited and scared him. At the last meeting, he thought perhaps they would finally get there.

Jane had sat next to him. Todd had sat frozen like a deer in the headlights for the entire hour and a half session. *What if she wants to talk?* He'd thought. *What do I say? God, she smells so good!* Todd need not have worried, though. Jane didn't say one word. When the meeting was over; she grabbed her stuff and flew out of the room as quickly as she could without so much as a backward glance.

Still, Todd viewed this encounter as progress in their relationship. He was determined to have a full conversation with her.

By the following Thursday, Todd had decided he was going to ask Jane out for coffee. Maybe what they needed to jump-start a conversation was a change of scenery. By Saturday, with some helpful nagging from his online friends, he finally found the courage to do it. He typed out and deleted countless drafts before he finally settled on a simple email message:

Hi Jane,
I was wondering if you would like to join me for coffee after the meeting this Tuesday. Just to talk. Would you be interested? I thought maybe we could go to the little coffee shop across the street. If you're available, let me know!
Todd

After sending the email, Todd couldn't focus on anything for the rest of the day. He had a very hard time sleeping that night. He would drift just to the edge of sleep, then suddenly bolt upright in his bed, convinced that he'd heard the familiar *ping!* that alerted him to new emails. The first time it happened, he had hopped right out of bed and hustled to his computer, only to discover that there wasn't any new email. He was very disappointed. After that, each time he thought he heard the sound, he would take deep calming breaths and repeat one of the meditation chants from S.M.A., "I am more than the sum of my online profiles. Technology doesn't define who I am; I have to power to hit the off switch. True happiness only exists outside of the chat room…" He would continue this for a few minutes, but eventually, hisresolve would crumble, and he would have to recheck his email before he could go back to sleep. Nothing there. By the time Monday morning came around, Todd was in a state of panic. She still hadn't responded to his email! He knew she was online; he could see her listed as online on the local chat group, but still no response. He didn't know what to do. Had she received the email? Was she angry with him? Should he say something? He was terrified that she would never talk to him again. By six o'clock that night,he decided to send her an apology in the hopes that he could somehow salvage their friendship. A desperate sliver of hope still remaining caused him to hit 'refresh' on his email one last time. There it was! A new email from Jane! His heart thudded in his chest as he opened it, both excited and apprehensive.

Hi Todd,
Sorry that I didn't respond right away. Your email came as a surprise. My sister Amy and I usually meet and go for coffee after the meetings. I would be delighted if you joined us. The coffee shop across the street is perfect. Seeyou tomorrow!
Jane

Tuesday night. Todd was excited! Coffee with Jane! He didn't think he'd ever been so nervous in his life. He changed his shirt three times before he was completely satisfied. He even decided to use a little cologne that his mother had bought him for Christmas. Unfortunately, his hands shook so badly that he ended up dumping nearly half the bottle on himself. After quickly showering and changing again, he left the house in a mad dash, desperate not to be late.

He got to the community center, where they held the meetings about an hour before the meeting was supposed to start. So he waited. As the minutes ticked by, he got more and more nervous. What if he couldn't do it? What if she thought he was boring? What if he freaked her out? What if, what if, what if? Finally, he couldn't sit still any longer, so he got out of the car and went into the building. He still had a full half-hour before the meeting was supposed to start, so he wandered around the lobby to pass the time. The community center was a large structure designed to accommodate a variety of group activities or meetings. The left side of the building held a moderate-size gym downstairs and a number of activity rooms upstairs designed for yoga, karate and dance classes. At the back of the building, there were a few psychiatrist offices, a chiropractor and a massage therapist. The right side of the building was geared to a more academic or business crowd. There were board rooms upstairs for business meetings and smaller classroom-style rooms downstairs for various workshops or group meetings. It was one of these rooms that they used for the
S.M.A. meetings, and it wasn't long before Todd found himself heading in that direction, simply out of habit.

As he approached the meeting room, he noticed the meeting facilitator, Andy, hanging a sign on the meeting room door. Todd liked Andy. He was easy to talk to. Andy was the type of guy who'd been there, done that and wasn't about to judge anyone. As Todd approached, Andy turned and smiled. "Hey, man! You're early today! Tell me, what do you think of this?" he asked, gesturing to the sign he had posted.

Social Media Anonymous –
Our goal is to help you unplug
In today's world, it is so easy to log onto many forms of social media. In fact, it is almost impossible to avoid. We are bombarded with a constant stream of information, entertainment and updates, all with the promise that we need it now, Now, NOW! It can be overwhelming. Our bodies require a certain amount of rest and relaxation that today's technologically fuelled society simply does not allow room for. Introducing the first-ever week-long media retreat, designed to teach you methods of relaxation and give you the tools you need to power down in your everyday life.
Note: Open to all S.M.A. members but must have approval from your therapist.

"Wow," said Todd, "a whole week?"

"That's right," said Andy, "I'll go over it in more detail at the end of the meeting." Andy looked Todd up and down and then grinned.

"You asked her out, didn't you?" Todd looked at the floor and turned an incredibly deep shade of red. "Good for you, Todd!" Andy gave Todd a reassuring pat on the shoulder as he passed him, heading toward the main doors to hang another sign.

Todd spent the next 20 minutes alternating between pacing the hall outside the meeting room and practicing what he was going to say to Jane. He jumped every time he heard the *whoosh!* of the main door opening down the hall. His heart would pound as he heard footsteps approaching. But each time, it wasn't her. Finally, it was time to start, and he had to go into the room.

***

"Well, we are just about out of time," said Andy. "I'd like to thank everyone for coming tonight, and thank you to those who shared your stories. Remember, we have to take it one day at a time. As you're leaving, please take an information pamphlet about the retreat. I know a week will be incredibly hard, but I believe you all have the strength to do it, and I challenge you to challenge yourselves. Let us end, as always, with our mantra."

All together, the group said, "Technology doesn't define who I am. I have the power to hit the off switch."

"Have a good week, everyone!" called Andy, as everyone began to gather their things and leave. Andy noticed Todd was taking his time and seemed disappointed. He had been watching the door for most of the meeting, looking less and less hopeful as time went by. *Damn Jane,* thought Andy, *where are you?* "Hey Todd, how's it going?"

"What did I do wrong? She isn't here. Why isn't she here? She said she would be here. What did I do to make her change her mind? It's just coffee! That's it. I don't know what to do!" Todd's voice got quieter and quieter until Andy had to strain to hear the last part, barely a whisper.

"How nervous were you about meeting her for coffee tonight?" asked Andy.

"Well…really nervous. I mean, she's…she's beautiful, funny and smart. I couldn't believe she said yes! I should have known it was too good to be true." Todd hung his head, defeated.

"Hang on just a minute," said Andy. "Don't you think that she's nervous too? Okay, maybe she did change her mind. But what if she's just really nervous? Maybe she's sitting at the coffee shop right now because both coming to the meeting and going to coffee would be too much for her. Why don't you go to the coffee shop and see if she's there? Come on, don't give up yet!"

Todd sighed. He just wanted to go home and put the whole nightmare behind him. Why did Andy have to make a valid point? That was annoying. Todd knew Jane. She would never intentionally hurt him like this. It was possible that she had been unable to handle both the meeting and coffee together. She was even less outgoing than he was, so he could see how she might feel that it was too much. He knew he had to at least check to see if she was there, if for no other reason than so when his online friends asked about tonight, he could tell them he had tried. "Okay, Andy. It's worth a try." Todd headed for the door, steeling himself for the worst.

***

Something was bothering Jane. No, not something, someone. That someone was Todd. He was like that annoyingly persistent mosquito that continually buzzes around your head while you're trying to sleep, all the while thinking *tomorrow I'm going to wake up with bites all over, I just know it!* It's not that Todd had done anything wrong exactly; it was just that Jane found him…interesting. Very interesting. That was very bad. Interesting was distracting, and Jane simply did not have the time to be distracted. She had work assignments, family obligations, projects to finish and yes, her social media 'hobby' that she was supposed to be cutting back on. No time for thinking about some Todd guy from S.M.A. Jane thought he was fun to chat with online, but she hadn't expected him to actually ask her to coffee after their next group meeting. They hadn't even said more than 'hello' in person, and now he was asking her to coffee? Jane couldn't remember the last time she had an IRL conversation with anyone other than her sister, Amy. The idea of it made it hard for her to breathe. She broke out into a cold sweat. No, no. No coffee. No getting to know each other in person. It was safer that way. Jane did the only thing she could think of. She ignored his email. She had been surprised to find tears stinging her eyes as she went through the familiar actions of blocking a friend on her various social media accounts. She had lost a fair number of good online friends in the last few years for the same reason. They just didn't understand that she didn't do IRL relationships. She didn't do relationships, period. No chance of getting hurt if you don't get involved. Still, it was a little harder to delete Todd. Jane had actually really liked him. *I should have known better than to start an online chat with someone from the group,* she thought. Too risky, not worth it. Jane decided she would skip her S.M.A. meeting to avoid any possible confrontation with Todd. Cowardly maybe, but Jane felt that distance would cement her desire to cease any further social interactions with Todd, online or otherwise.

Having no desire to explain to her sister why she was skipping a meeting, she had simply met Amy at their usual spot around the time the meeting was over. Jane didn't want Amy to worry that she was quitting her meetings. Jane had just wanted to go right home, but Amy had insisted that they stop for coffee first. They'd taken their drinks to a cozy table in the corner of the coffee shop opposite the door. After a few minutes, Jane could tell something was wrong. Amy was quiet. Amy didn't do quiet. She usually chatted on about work, asked Jane about hers, and regaled Jane with tales of all the silly things that had happened inthe last week. Today, however, Amy was acting a little off. At first, Jane was worried that Amy had realized that she had skipped out on her S.M.A. meeting. After a few more minutes of sitting in silence, Jane decided that no, Amy didn't seem angry or upset she was acting more like she was nervous. Every time the door opened, Amy would look up, then return to slowly shredding a napkin. "Amy, is something bothering you?" Amy looked up, surprised, and then her face crumpled into a sob.

"I'm so sorry! Please promise me you won't get upset! I shouldn't have snooped; I was just worried about you! They told me to monitor your internet usage as part of your counselling program, which I have been doing. Normally all I do is log the amount of time; I swear I don't check on everything you do. But this time, I noticed the name Todd and I recognize it because you mentioned a Todd in your group, and I just wanted to see if it was that Todd and I read his email, and I knew you just ignored it because it didn't show a reply. I worry about you because you spend so much time alone and when you were talking about him it sounded like you really like him. You never give yourself a chance to be happy, and you really should, so I emailed him and told him to meet us here, and I know you're angry, and I'm really sorry!"

Amy said all this is one big rush with her face hidden behind her hands, sobbing uncontrollably. It took Jane almost two full minutes to figure out exactly what Amy was saying. Then Jane felt like crying herself. It was suddenly incredibly hard to breath. She could actually feel her throat restricting, and she could only get a little air into her lungs.

"Take. Me. Home. NOW!" Jane said.

"Too late. Isn't that him?" asked Amy, nodding toward the door. Jane turned in her chair and saw Todd standing in the doorway, scanning the room for her. Jane quickly turned back before he looked her way, and glared at her sister. "Come on, Jane! Give him a chance. Give yourself a chance!"

"No, Amy, really, I just want to go. Can we just… "

"Hey Todd!" Amy said loudly, waving to get his attention. "Over here!" Jane concentrated on getting air into her lungs as Todd made his way through the now crowded coffee shop to their table. "Hi Todd, I'm Amy, Jane's sister. It's so nice to meet you!" Amy stood and shook Todd's hand and offered him her chair. "Why don't you sit right here, Todd. I'm going to order myself another drink. Can I get you something? Coffee?"

"Um, s-sure…that would be great. Thanks," stammered Todd.

"No problem," Amy turned to Jane, "What about you, sis?" Jane didn't respond. She just continued to glare at Amy. "Er…okay then. I'll be right back." Amy pushed her way through the crowd to the end of the line.

Todd and Jane exchanged nervous smiles. They sat in silence. The minutes ticked by. Silence. Todd started a million conversations in his mind, but the words seemed to die in his throat before he could get them out. Every so often, it would look like Jane was about to say something, but then she seemed to change her mind, looking away, cheeks flushed. It was frustrating! How was it they could talk for hours online but couldn't have a single conversation in person? He wished they had a computer right now so he could tell her how thrilled he was that she was with him. All that was on the table, though, was an empty coffee mug and napkins.

Suddenly, Todd had an idea. He took a pen from his pocket and grabbed a napkin. He wrote on the napkin. *Hi, my name is Todd.* He added a smiley face and then folded it and slid the note across the table to Jane. Looking a bit puzzled, Jane took the note and read it. She laughed out loud, and it was the most wonderful sound Todd had ever heard.

Jane took a deep, steadying breath, smiled and said, "Hi, my name is Jane."

Kristoffer Law

Kristoffer Law has been an avid reader since the age of three, and his love of the written word is boundless. He began work on his first novel, *The Jagged Tree,* in April 2011 and completed first draft work on it in October 2013. Work on the second novel in the series, *The 4th Wall*, began in August 2014. Kristoffer currently lives in Victoria, BC, with his cross-eyed tabby Jana.

Happy Anniversary

This is it, Herbert thought to himself. Time to set it right. He peeled himself slowly out of his threadbare recliner and pushed himself to his feet with shaking hands. His knees offered their usual grievances as he shuffled across the living room toward the kitchen. He stood in the doorway, his tired eyes roaming over the spotless counters and empty sink. He tried to remember the last time it had been this clean and could not; in fact, he distinctly recalled having somewhat of an argument the night before with a large can of beef stew. The electric can opener had gotten stuck about two-thirds of the way through and the can had slipped unceremoniously out of its magnetic grasp to crash onto the peeling linoleum. He remembered watching helplessly as sauce and flecks of beef and vegetables spewed onto the floor and across the cabinet doors in front of the sink. He'd started to clean it up, but his knees and back had refused to partake and in the end he'd left it to harden overnight while he ate a bag of salt'n'vinegar potato chips for dinner.

There wasn't a speck of food or dirt anywhere in the kitchen now, and he puzzled over it for a few moments. At last he nodded quietly to himself as he reached the only conclusion that seemed to make sense. Vera cleaned it up. Had to have done. His lips thinned. Today they'd been married 62 years, and after all he'd done – things like leaving beef stew to congeal overnight – he'd best do right by her now. And he had it all planned out. A bottle of red wine sat chilling in the spare fridge in the garage. He had bought it almost two weeks earlier, sneaking off to the liquor store while on his daily walk. The detour took him almost a half mile further than he should have gone, and his body screamed at him for the next three days because of it, but carrying that bottle home put such a smile on his face that he couldn't remove it. The best part was she had no idea. Vera never went into the garage unless it was absolutely necessary.

He moved slowly into the heart of the kitchen, going through the steps of his plan again in his mind. He would make a picnic lunch, like he'd seen in so many old movies. Cold chicken, various cheeses, sliced apples, some stoned wheat thin crackers, and of course the red wine. Putting it all together, he reckoned, should give him slightly less of a headache than the beef stew. The perfect picnic, he thought. The perfect date. He smiled to himself at the prospect of leading her by the hand out the door, the wicker basket hanging from his free arm by its handle, the checkered tablecloth sticking partway out from under one of the basket flaps like a red and white tongue. He thought about her laugh tinkling merrily in chorus with the wine glasses in the basket, the sweet summer breeze dancing playfully with the hem of her sundress. The perfect date, for the perfect wife. His smile broadened into the same schoolboy grin he bore when he'd bought the wine.

He started humming under his breath as he pulled out the first of the assortment of cheeses from the fridge. As he started peeling away the cling film that encased the marble cheddar, it began to crumble away into dust as the air hit it. In his panic, his hands began to tremble as he unwrapped it faster. The more the cheese was exposed, the quicker it became dust before his eyes. He lost his grip on the end of the block and the cheese flew up into the air, unraveling itself as it tumbled end over end through the air. As it landed on the cold linoleum, the clear film seemed to split in dozens of places. The cheese blew apart into a fine cloud upon impact, hanging in the air for several seconds before settling irretrievably across the opposite counter and the floor in front of it. Herbert stood staring at the cling film as it settled in on itself somewhat, his mouth agape.

"No," he whispered. "No…" He took a step forward and then stopped. He closed his eyes, and his lower lip quivered a little. He rocked back and forth on his feet. It's just one block, he thought. One of three. He turned back to the fridge and opened it, reaching for the remaining blocks of white and yellow cheddar. His fingers clawed at the empty space on the glass shelf where the cheese had lain. They were just here a minute ago! he thought. Indeed they had, stacked like bricks one on top of the other, the marble on top…except now one was obliterated and the other two had disappeared.

"What the hell…?" he said to himself. He closed the fridge door. He counted to ten and re-opened it. If he looked hard enough he could almost see the cheese, a ghostly echo on the shelf. He closed the door a second time and turned away from it, his face sullen. He'd wanted everything to be perfect, and now this. Vera loved – absolutely LOVED – marble cheddar, and he remembered being so pleased at seeing the cheese on sale at the grocer's just the week before.

Now he felt oddly alone in the kitchen as he turned back to the refrigerator once again. I'm going to open it, he thought. And it WILL be there. All of it. He opened the door with the zeal of a gunslinger whipping his pistol out during a draw in the old dust dramas he used to watch as a young man. The door groaned on its hinges, and the fridge actually shifted forward about three inches from the force of the pull. When he peered inside, however, the cheese still wasn't there. Even the ghost image of it had disappeared. He shut the door and turned away, his lips thin and his head shaking. What to do?

The roast chicken he'd bought sat in the sparefridge in the garage, along with the wine. He could still manage the picnic without the cheese. He gathered up the pieces of cling film from the counter and the floor and tossed them into the garbage underneath the sink, and then began his slow shuffle down the hall to the garage entrance.

The garage was chilly, even on a warm day like today, and musty. A thin layer of dust lay over everything, including the 1989 LeBaron neither of them had driven in nearly fifteen years. The sparefridge sat in a corner just to the right of his old workbench; a silent, gunmetal monolith that had seen the rise and fall of Hitler's armies and still operated some 70 years later. Herbert shuffled over to it now, kicking up tiny clouds of dust and wood shavings as he went. He grasped the pull handle and gave a tug, and the door refused to open. His brows knotted together in the middle of his forehead, and he tightened his grip. A second tug and the door reluctantly relented, a small psssh sound coming with it, like a soda bottle being opened. He stepped aside to allow the door to swing fully open, and let his breath out in a long sigh. The cheese had left him half-expecting the chicken and wine to be no more, but there they sat, the wine on the top shelf and the chicken underneath.

He removed the chicken first, the cold air emanating from inside the fridge making the hair on the back of his hands stand to attention. He could see the chicken through the clear plastic dome lid, a rich, savoury brown. He smiled a little, and put the chicken down on the work bench before turning back to collect the wine. The chill of the glass bottle caused him to almost drop it as he pulled it out, and he quickly brought his right hand up to hold it steady from the bottom. I lost the cheese, he thought. But I'll be damned if I lose the wine. He set the wine down next to the chicken, and had just turned again to close the door when he heard an odd sound, like someone crumpling up crisp cellophane. He turned back to the work bench, the fridge door forgotten, and saw something terrible. The chicken, sitting in a beam of sunlight coming in through a dirty window, was now in the process of turning into a green, viscous sludge in the bottom of the tray. His eyes widened in confusion and anger.

"NO!" he cried. "You son of a..." His words stopped short on the tip of his tongue as he pried off the clear plastic dome. Like the cheese in the kitchen, the introduction of fresh air only sped up the decomposition process, and within seconds all that was left was a murky green soup an inch thick in the bottom of the tray.

"NO!" he shouted again, and picked up the tray, hurling it like a Frisbee across the garage. It turned upside down in mid-air and landed on the old LeBaron, splattering green muck across the hood. "YOU BASTARD!" he cried. His face worked as he stared at the mess on his car, his eyes sparkling with rage. After a long moment, he turned back to the work bench, bringing his fist down upon its surface hard. The thud of his hand sounded flat in the silence, and a cloud of sawdust plumed up into the air, provoking a series of fitful sneezes. When everything had settled, he regarded the wine sitting stoically on the table, freshdust just beginning to coat its neck. His eyes narrowed. Please, if nothing else, let the wine be untouched, he thought.

He carried the wine delicately like a newborn back into the kitchen. He set it down on the counter by the toaster, far enough from the edge that he was satisfied there would be no risk of further accidents. He leaned up against the sink and pushed his glasses up on his forehead, rubbing his eyes and trying to think a way out of this mess.

Half his picnic menu was gone. How the hell am I supposed to manage this now? he thought. He looked at the clock above the stove and saw that it was already two-thirty in the afternoon. Far too late to attempt a walk to the store to get more supplies. He set his glasses down on his nose again and let out another long sigh. Chicken and cheese, both gone. All that was left was the crackers, apples and wine. Not much of a picnic. Fear filled him. The speed of the disintegration of the roast chicken and the cheese (not to mention the out-and-out disappearance of the other two blocks) was fantastic in the truest sense of the word, and set his body into chilled shivers. He couldn't remember ever seeing anything like it. He looked again at the clock. There was no time to fuss over what had already happened. He had to salvage what he could and make the best of it.

He opened the cupboard above the sink and pulled down a small Tupperware dish with a lid. On the shelf just below it, he pulled down the package of stoned wheat thins, and placed both on the counter. Please, he begged. Please let this and the rest of the food I put together remain intact. That's all I want; just let me have this day with my wife. Please I'll do anything if you'll just let me have that. Never much of a church- goer, he stopped himself mid-thought. Bargaining with God? Add this to the list of things he couldn't believe, please. Just moments ago he was almost ungovernably angry and now he was standing here in his kitchen, at 86 years old, pleading silently with something he'd never believed in in the first place.

He opened the package of thins, holding his breath as he did so. After a long moment, he peered into the box and saw that the crackers were untouched and intact. Mad relief filled him in a rush. He tentatively shook a couple out into the Tupperware dish, and let his breath out in a whoosh as they clacked harmlessly into the plastic container. A small miracle! he thought. No chicken or cheese, but by golly we'll have the finest crackers and wine in the history of all picnics! He giggled out loud to himself, a strange, chirrupy sound, empty and hollow in the silence of the kitchen. He found the lid and secured it on the top of the dish. One down, one to go.

He padded softly over to the fruit bowl and selected two apples. He brought them back over to the cutting board and began slicing the first one down the middle. One half of the apple fell away, rocking back and forth on the cutting board, and in its center Herbert saw something small and twitching. He looked to the half that he held in his hand and dropped the knife on the floor, the tip of the blade burying itself in the linoleum barely half an inch from his slippered foot. Three maggots, fat and shiny, were wriggling in the meat of the apple around its core. A fourth without its head fell out onto the cutting board, twitching blindly back and forth. A scream crouched down at the back of his throat, readying itself for the inevitable launch that would propel it beyond his lips, but at the last minute he clamped his jaw shut hard enough to rattle his dentures. He snatched up the second apple, moving to throw it in the trash under the sink. The apple's skin was dry and tight, and in the few seconds it was in his hand, he could swear he could feel something – indeed, several somethings – wriggling and squirming just below his fingertips. As the apple tumbled from his hand in the waste bin, the scream in his throat turned into a deep growl-groan, and he wiped his fingers furiously on the front of his slacks without thinking. He turned and yanked the cutting board up off the counter. The maggoty half of the apple teetered and almost fell on the floor, but he managed to right the board at the last minute. The apple half toppled over on its face, the top edge landing on the headless maggot still wriggling stupidly in the middle of the board. The larva popped up in theair and Herbert shoved the board away from him instinctively. By a small miracle, both halves crashed into the waste bin, but two of the maggots did not. They landed on the floor with a small plop and wriggled crazily. He dropped the cutting board on top of them and brought a slippered foot down hard. He could hear two tiny pops, almost feeling them through the board and his slipper. Revulsion filled him for the better part of ten minutes.

He turned back to the Tupperware dish of crackers sitting next to the bottle of wine and frowned, thinking it all a very meager picnic indeed. He scratched his head, trying to think of alternatives he could add, and for a moment came up blank. Then it came to him: he could heat up another can of the beef stew Vera kept in the pantry just down the hall. One of those would make the meal a bit more rounded. He walked down the hall to the pantry. He pulled a can down from the shelf and regarded it for a moment. Just heat andserve. Easy as pie.

Back in the kitchen, he turned the stovetop onbefore pulling the electric can opener out from the wall and placing the can in its magnetic grip. He pushed the On button and barely had time to collect a saucepan from the dish-rack before there was a small but audible thump! and the kitchen descended into dusky silence. His eyes snapped to the can opener to see the can barely a quarter of the way open, frozen in place. The small red glow of the stovetop element was already fading, and when he looked up towards the clock, all that greeted him was a blank, black face.

A blown fuse, that's all it is, he reassured himself. He was not confident, however, and he shook his head. You don't think so? his inner voice chided. Check the other rooms and see for yourself then. Start with the VCR in the living room. If it's a breaker, the VCR will still be on.

He moved with determination into the living room and stood in front of the entertainment unit. The VCR clock was blank. Then a voice, from down the hall.

"Herb? What happened?"

Vera.

He cleared his throat before speaking. "Nothing, Vera. Looks like just a power outage." He glanced outside but saw nothing along the avenue that would back up his claim. His response seemed to have settled the matter for his wife, however, as she didn't follow up with more questions. Check the breaker, his inner voice goaded. Just to be sure. He nodded in agreement. The breaker. Sure. The entire house's power is shut down from one little can opener. He shook his head and found himself making deals in his head once again. God, I hope it's just a breaker. All I wanted was this day and it's all going to hell in a hand basket. Just give me this one little thing.

He entered the garage once more and opened the fuse box that sat on the wall just inside the door. The sunlight pouring in through the windows allowed him to see the switches easily, and all of them were in the ON position. Not one breaker was tripped. Well, there you go, he thought. With all the breakers as they should be, a power outage seemed most likely. Heslumped his shoulders. All his plans, all his hopes,were beyond salvaging now. He turned to go back inside the house and shuffled dejectedly over to his easy chair. He fell into it with a groan, and rested his head on the back of the chair, his eyelids barely holding back tears.

Sixty-two years and all he wanted was to take his wife outside and see her smile at him in the sunlight like she had when they were first courting. When the war had just ended, and life was returning to normal. He wanted a picnic like they'd shared when he proposed to her, and now he had nothing. The first tear broke free of its eyelash prison and scurried down his face unheeded. All for nothing, he thought. Nothing, nothing… He opened his eyes and looked through prisms of tears at the field that lay next to their house; the field where he planned to take Vera and share in this day with her. Their anniversary. Theirlove.

Vera walked into the kitchen like a ghost, and looked at the food her husband had collected on the counter. She turned and looked in on him sitting in hischair as he stared out the window before looking back at the crackers and wine. She smiled. Without a word, and without a sound, she went back down the hallway to a small closet and pulled out their old picnic basket and the red and white checkered tablecloth that went with it. She draped the folded cloth over her arm and carried the basket back to the kitchen. She glanced at him one more time before setting everything down on the counter. Herb was still staring morosely out the window.

brought down two wine glasses from the shelf and placed the dish of crackers into the basket. She placed the wine glasses in the basket carefully, wrapping them in cloth napkins as she did so. The wine and corkscrew went in last, padded and protected with more cloths, and after she closed the lid of the basket she threaded the checkered table cloth through the handle. She tested its weight before lifting it completely off the counter, and then walked with it under her arm intothe living room.

Herb hadn't heard his wife's movements through anything that she did in the kitchen, and turned from the window in surprise at the sound of her voice speaking his name.

"I…" was all he could manage. As the sun glowed on her face from the window, she looked to him as she had all those years ago when they were both young. Young and in love, with the whole of the worldbefore them. Another tear tripped down his cheek, butthis one was borne of happiness. He looked down and saw the picnic basket and looked back up at her, and began an attempt to explain.

"Shhh," she said. "What you did is perfect. Let's enjoy the day, just you and me. We never needed much to be happy together. Why should today be any different?" She smiled at him and moved off to the door, slipped on a pair of shoes, then turned back to him, her face expectant. "What are you waiting for?" she asked. "The afternoon won't last forever!"

He eased himself carefully out of his recliner, smiling a little more to himself again. Maybe it's not as bad as all that, he thought to himself. Maybe she's right – all we really needed was each other. She opened the door as he crossed over to where she stood, not bothering to change out of his slippers as he walked outside into the fresh air. He slowly navigated the stone steps down to the field edge, which lapped against the bottom stair like water. The breeze was light and cheery on his face, and he could smell the faint scent of lilacs from the field. He looked up into the sky, his smile broadening. This is a perfect day. A perfect day for me and my wife. He paused a moment and watched Vera walk ahead of him a few yards, himself rocking a little unsteadily on his feet. The grass, ankle-high here, seemed to whisper to itself in barely-contained excitement. Another light zephyr caressed him around his middle, rippling his clothes as it encircled him playfully. Vera turned back to look at him, and then extended her hand to him.

"Come on, Herb. Over here, by the brook. Come sit with me!" she said, laughing. He laughed back, an easy, fluid chuckle that was youthful and free. He closed the distance between them and reached out, grasping her hand in his, the warmth of her body filling him up with pure joy. A perfect day. A perfect picnic. I love you, Vera.

***

The flies abandoned the beef stew three days after it first splattered across the floor and cupboard doors. The air was still and close in the old house, the temperature inexorably rising into the mid-thirties in the time since Herbert Parkins passed away in his easy chair. A half-eaten bag of salt'n'vinegar potato chips sat in the crook of his arm, crumbs resting in the chesthair that sprouted up from behind the open collar of his shirt. In his other hand he clutched a framed photograph of his wife Vera. Vera, who had died of Alzheimer's some seven years earlier. Even as death overtook him, a smile could be seen on Herbert's face. A smile which, even now, reached all the way to the corners of his eyes.

And somewhere, beyond his eyelids, beyond his memory, Herbert sat down next to his wife Vera and cracked open the bottle of red wine. And somewhere beyond this world, Herb and Vera sat and drank and laughed and fell in love all over again.

Monique Jacob

Monique Jacob is the author of *Tye Dye Voodoo* and its sequel, *Voodoo Mystery Tour*, the saga of Cricket Lake and how magic and intrigue transformed a BC Interior town into an unexpected tourist mecca. Go to www.moniquejacob.com for free downloads of excerpts and deleted scenes.

"First Responder" is a new short story written just for this Anthology and shows us how death is not necessarily a barrier to love.

"Mrs. Kwan" is a scene from Monique's upcoming novel *Global Swarming,* in which a traumatized population redefines what binds communities together.

First Responder

Annie heard someone call her name. She opened her eyes to thick, billowing smoke on all sides. The fire! Her heart beat frantically and she crouched, making herself smaller. She clapped a hand to her mouth, too late to prevent the intake of breath she needed to give voice to her panic.

But she did not scream. She froze instead, confused by the sweet taste that breath had left on her tongue. Not the burning, acrid smoke she had expected.

Annie had lost track of her mother, who'd been clutching her hand as they blindly groped through the fire that had engulfed their shared quarters. Her mother would be terrified, and Annie turned back to where she last remembered feeling the touch of her mother's fingers.

Annie heard her name again. She felt dizzy as she spun to face the voice, staring into the dense whiteness she had mistaken for smoke. She could not see her outstretched hand before her, and anyone could have been standing just past her fingertips.

She shouted for help but her words were a whisper that barely made it past her lips. Could she have imagined hearing her name? Was it all in her mind? Her thoughts were muddled, as if her head were filled with the same thick mist that flowed and twisted around her. It appeared to have little substance, disturbing neither her hair nor her skirts as it passed.

Annie remembered those skirts afire and her mother's burning hair throwing sparks in her face. She sank to the floor and wrapped her arms around herself.

"Annie!"

Her head snapped up and she glimpsed a man's face through the rolling whiteness. He wavered in and out of sight, a shifting apparition, but his eyes were locked on hers. He could see her!

"There she is! Right there in front of me!"

Cliff pointed at a spot several inches above the floor. He looked up at the others, all of whom were staring at him except Brent, who gaped at the spot Cliff was indicating. The blood had drained from his face.

"G-ghost." Brent gulped audibly and fled, trampling bandages, splints, and other first aid supplies the four of them had scattered throughout the room during the last emergency scenario.

"C'mon guys, how could you miss her?" Cliff paced the area, eyeing the spot on the floor from every angle. "She was looking right at me."

"All I saw was a little puff of steam, like your breath when it's cold out. Doesn't exactly count as a ghost, though you might want to talk to Brent about what he saw." Rob grinned and waved out the window at Brent, who was trying to jam his key into his car door's lock without much success.

"Well, she's trespassing," Leo said as he turned off the oxygen tanks. "You're security around here, so she's your problem."

"Ghosts are not in my job description," Cliff said and waved a hand through the air where he'd seen the wispy figure.

"They also don't have anything to do with first aid. Help me clean this mess up so I can get out of here." Leo rolled a tensor bandage and snugged it into the corner of his jump kit. He gathered up the first aid report forms they'd been practicing on and tossed them into the recycling bin along with two empty glove boxes and a handful of bandage wrappers.

"She shows up when I'm practicing CPR on one of the Annies, but only if I actually play the role and talk to the doll," Cliff said musingly. "This is the third time I've seen her this week."

"So, you're saying your ghost's name is Annie?"

Cliff squatted and laid a palm on the spot where he'd seen her appear. It was no warmer or cooler than the rest of the floor. "I don't know what I'm saying. All I know is that if I make like I really mean to save the Annie doll, then I see the ghost."

He stacked the CPR dummy with her identical sisters, wondering who had named them all Annie, and when. Cliff hadn't thought to ask until now. The Annies all wore t-shirts with the *First Responder* logo but in different colours. There were no other distinguishing features between the dolls except for those colours. They all had the same plastic hairdo, the same featureless eyes and gaping mouth. Some of the guys had made jokes about those open mouths at first but practicing artificial respiration on those inert plastic victims made them a lot less sexy.

Cliff had worked nights as a security guard in the building for two years. He'd never seen so much as a whisper of a ghost until *First Responder* moved in and took over a good portion of the main floor. The school offered special discounts to the tenants andstaff in the building, and Cliff's boss hinted that first aid training would go far in advancing his career. Cliff knew the boss was joking but he could barely get a Band-Aid out of its wrapper without contaminating it, so a little training couldn't hurt.

Cliff set the alarm after Rob and Leo left, andjogged to the security office at the back of the building. He started a pot of coffee and changed into his uniform while it brewed. His routine was the same,every shift. Four times a night he walked the hallways, common areas and stairwells inside the building, followed by a full sweep of the grounds and parking lot.

Cliff didn't really care about advancing his career. He was pretty content right where he was, working fulltime with two weeks in summer to fish and a week in fall to chop wood and get his mother's house ready forsnow. It was a peaceful job most nights, with only a few homeless folks and their dogs digging in the coffee shop dumpster for leftovers, or looking for a safe corner to bed down.

His steps echoed as he strode around to the front of the building. It was three a.m. and the temperature was dropping. He kept an eye out for daytime puddles that were now glistening black patches of slipperiness, just waiting for him to hit their icy surfaces at the wrong angle and break his neck.

Cliff paused at *First Responder*'s front window, peering into its shadowy depths to the jumble of plastic torsos. Headlights beamed across the lot as a car passed, lighting the inside of the classroom for a moment. They reflected off the fake skin-tone of an Annie doll. He wondered if this was the specific doll he'd been working on when he'd seen the ghost tonight.

"Annie," he whispered. His breath fogged the glass and he almost missed the ghostly wisp that formed for a moment on the other side of the window. It dissipated quickly, but he was certain he'd seen a trace of her face again. Was she haunting the first aid school or the building itself – or him?

He cut his round short and headed back to the office. He was freezing anyway. He turned up the heat and switched the main computer from surveillance monitoring to the internet.

Cliff hardly knew where to start but a simple search using the words *ghost* and *Mason Street* brought up an old newspaper account of a fire on the site in 1947.

The building had burned to the ground and two people had died: Margaret Spruce and her daughter Annie.

John Spruce had owned a successful tailoring shop, living with his family in the flat above. When he died, most of his clients went across town to his competitor and Margaret nearly lost the business until she and Annie moved into the back room and rented out the top floor to pay the bills.

There was a grainy black and white photo of Annie and her parents standing in front of *Spruce's Tailoring*. She was a solemn young woman with long wavy hair.

Cliff printed the photo on the office's old machine. The resulting image of Annie was even fuzzier, as if it had been taken of her ghostly counterpart and not her living self. Her eyes were dark smudges that tilted upward at the corners. He set the print of Annie on the desk.

Another search brought up a pair of photographs of the street where the tailor shop had stood, before and after. The second photo showed a gap in the street where three buildings had burned. The space looked to be about the size of the current building, which went up barely a year after the fire.

Annie was twenty-four when she died, six years younger than Cliff. Even across a gulf of nearly seventy years and with nothing more than a crappy photocopy of a grainy black and white photo, Cliff would have liked to meet Annie Spruce.

He sometimes wished he been born in simpler times and smiled as he thought of how he would have had to approach her stern-faced father just to take her for a walk or to a picnic. It might be easier to ask someone for a date these days, but courting a tailor's daughter sounded like a slice of heaven.

Cliff stroked a finger across the blurry face. Annie stood taller than her mother and leaned toward her as if she were about to say something. He'd seen her three times now, each successive appearance more distinct than the last. Would she appear even more clearly if he continued to call her?

He pushed away his coffee mug and sighed. Time to finish his rounds. He switched the system back to surveillance and nearly knocked the mug off the desk. The monitor showed two shadowy forms in the coffee shop. Cliff glanced left, at a blinking red light that was the building's silent alarm. No telling how long it had been flashing.

He cursed and got to his feet, snagging his cell phone so he could call the police on the way. He hadn't meant to be online for so long, but thieves didn't usually come snooping around when it was this cold.

An icy wind blasted into the office as Cliff opened the door. It fluttered the papers on the desk and he snatched the printout of Annie's photo before it hit the floor. He folded it carefully so as not to crease her face and shoved it into an inside pocket. He turned up his collar and slapped a hand onto his uniform cap when the wind threatened to take it.

He was surprised by how much of the forecasted snow had already fallen. Everything in sight was covered in white. Cliff carefully picked his way to the front of the building, walking on the frozen grass verge where the footing was less treacherous. He heard a muffled curse and saw one of the thieves swing a crowbar through the front window of *First Responder*. The noise was deafening and Cliff was surprised that no one sleeping upstairs in the condos had called the police when the first door had been smashed.

Cliff pressed his back against the building as he closed the gap between him and the shards of glass lying in the trampled snow on the walkway. He could hear two men arguing as they noisily pulled everything out of the well-stocked first aid supply cabinets.

They were probably looking for drugs and too stupid or stoned to see that it wasn't a real pharmacy. Cliff approached carefully. Junkies didn't tend to carry guns but it was that sort of thinking that could get him shot.

Most of the glass was gone from the front door of *First Responder*, with only a few jagged pieces left clinging to the frame. Cliff carefully peered around the corner and saw a dark form racing toward him. He jerked his head back but not fast enough to avoid the second man, who threw his shoulder into Cliff, driving him against the door frame where a lethal shard of glass skewered the right side of his neck.

Cliff's mouth opened in a silent scream, and he heard the two laughing like idiots as they escaped, unaware that they'd left him impaled. His hands came up and he gently touched the shard of glass that was buried in his throat. Hot blood spurted over his fingers and pattered on the fresh snow at his feet.

Part of his mind was numb from shock and horror while another part calmly assessed the scene as he'd been trained to do. First rule of squirting blood was to apply pressure – which contradicted the rule that said never pull out the stabby object.

Cliff tried to calm his rising gibbering fear at the sight of his blood melting so much snow. He closed his eyes so he wouldn't have to see all that red, and then his legs gave out and he slipped to the ground, pulling away from the glass dagger.

He hardly noticed that he'd fallen, except that his left cheek was cold where it lay on the ground and there were snowflakes tickling his nose. He dragged a hand along the ground to his chest and pressed it against his coat, where the photo of Annie sat in his pocket, warm against his heart. He whispered her name as he lost consciousness and thought he heard her voice in return.

A warm hand against his cold cheek made him shiver and he opened his eyes, relieved that help had finally arrived. The snow had thickened and he could barely see his surroundings, let alone the face of his rescuer.

"It's all right. I'm here."

He blinked hard, and the dense whiteness that he now realized wasn't snow parted to show a familiar face. Annie's hair drifted around her shoulders and shesmiled when she saw that he'd recognized her.

He lifted a trembling hand to his neck but felt no blood and no gaping tear in his skin. He was dead. He shivered and gazed in amazement at Annie, *his* first responder, as she took his hand and helped him to his feet. He could hardly feel the ground they were standing on, but her touch was solid and he clutched her hand as he stared at the face he'd first glimpsed only a few days ago.

Her eyes were pale blue and matched the blouse she wore over her darker blue skirt. She looked exactly the same age as in the photograph. His heart was still racing but with a different emotion than fear, and he nearly stumbled when she tugged at his hand and led him through the rolling mists. Cliff laughed in delight and followed his love into this new adventure.

Mrs. Kwan

The truck jostled and bounced on the rutted road. Mrs. Kwan flinched as another low-hanging branch cracked against the windshield like a whip.

"Don't worry, Ma," Gus said. He was bent low over the steering wheel so he could peer through the dense greenery. "That windshield is made of two sheets of glass reinforced with high-tensile stainlesssteel. It's as strong as your toughest soup pot."

Mrs. Kwan squinted at the glass, trying to catch the glint of steel. She glanced at Gus. The corner of his mouth was twitching.

"How did I have the bad luck to birth such a son?" she asked, slapping his arm. "Only you would test your poor mother's patience with idiotic jokes at a time like this."

Gus held up his arm in mock defense, grinning widely. He was glad to see her so feisty. She'd been quiet for most of the trip, gazing out the window with an expression that didn't change whether they were passing a roadside tent city housing thousands, or a river of red fire ants swarming a field of bloated cow carcasses. Gus was so relieved she'd finally left the mosquito-infested Flats that he had filled the silence with constant chatter about Red Fort and its community.

He watched his mother dig through her enormous tote bag, probably looking for another tissue-wrapped sandwich. She'd already pulled out a stack of them for Dave and Jeff back at the last check point. Gus had expected her to freak out when they arrived at the gate and those two brutes came crashing out of the woods on either side of the road with their rifles pointing at the truck's windows.

But they had dropped all attitude when they encountered the tiny Asian woman in the passenger seat. She pulled out food and they became like devoted puppies, waving the truck through.

"Tell me again about this girl, Jin-Ho."

"Come on, Ma. I've told you a billion times. Don't call me that."

"You bought her from a gang of bikers and now she's the love of your life."

"Someone else bought Miranda but now he's dead and she's free to be with whoever she wants to."

"Your sister knows some nice Korean girls."

Gus rolled his eyes and willed himself not to bang his head against the steering wheel. Hundreds of miles with nothing to say and now she wanted to play matchmaker. "Miranda's a nice normal girl who was going to teacher's college when the world went to crap. We've all had it rough and she's no different."

"But you said she has orphans, not even her own children. Where are their parents?"

"They're *all* orphans, Ma."

The truck rounded a bend and the road widened into an enormous flat field, where at least a dozen people stopped working to watch their arrival. A boy and a dog raced across the field to meet the truck.

Gus geared down and the truck groaned as it slowed and finally stopped. It was fully loaded thistime and he'd felt the weight of it over his shoulder with every mile they covered on their way up the province. His mother had insisted on bringing everything she owned, which was a lot considering her many years running the Hope Trading Post. Gus had told her she would never be coming back.

The tide was receding, again, in its new pattern of seasonal surges. In a month they'd be salvaging all the way out to the old Richmond airport, driving the treacherous sodden concrete roads and hoping a washout wouldn't leave them stranded. The Flats would also become host to fresh swarms of mosquitos in millions of stagnant pools and the malaria camps would fill up again. Gus might only get one moresalvage trip this time but moving his mother out of there had been first priority.

More people were coming out of the woods from the many paths that led away from the main field. They closed in on the truck, smiling and waving. Mrs. Kwan's eye was drawn to a woman carrying a childthat clung to her like a little monkey.

Gus followed her gaze. "Miranda's the one holding Kia, and remember that Marty is only eight. Be nice." He set the brake and opened the door just as Marty arrived with Rug, in a flurry of shouting and barking.

Mrs. Kwan paused for a moment, watching her son as he greeted these strangers she'd heard so much about. She stepped out of the truck as Miranda reached them. Gus whispered to Marty, who ran to take Kia from Miranda's arms.

Marty carried his sister over to stand a few feet from Mrs. Kwan. The dog sat next to him, panting heavily and sweeping the ground with its tail. It was missing fur in large patches and smelled awful but the boy didn't flinch when the dog leaned against his legs. A well-loved dog would be protective of its boy, Mrs. Kwan noted approvingly.

"They're gonna be kissing for a while," Marty said. "It's disgusting."

Mrs. Kwan glanced to the side and saw both children watching her with interest. The little girl was firmly attached to her brother, with her head resting on his bony shoulder. "That's a rude thing to say. Being rude gets many chores."

Marty stared at her incredulously. "You can't tell me what to do." Kia stirred in his arms and he nearly dropped her as she loosened her grip and reached for the old woman.

"Talking back gets even more chores," Mrs. Kwan replied, taking Kia from her brother. Though the child was at least three, she weighed hardly more than a cat and Mrs. Kwan wondered if she could walk.

"Quit while you're ahead, buddy," Gus called over Miranda's shoulder, which earned a laugh from everyone on the field.

Marty folded his arms over his skinny chest and squinted at Mrs. Kwan suspiciously. Kia had wrapped herself around Gus's mom as if she already knew her.

Marty shuffled a step closer. "What do I get if I'm good?"

Mrs. Kwan eyed the boy. He had seen his parents killed by swarms of red fire ants and was very protective of his little sister, yet he hadn't flinched when a stranger took her from his arms. Marty would trust her because he trusted Gus. She put a hand on his head and stroked his sun-warmed hair.

"You get a grandmother."

Pam Desjardine

Pam was born in Whitehorse, Yukon Territory in the mid-'50s. She followed her parents around to various communities until just before she turned six, moving to Edmonton with her mom and two sisters. They gained a step-dad and relocated to the interior of BC just three short years later.

Raised earth-honouring, Pam's journey of self-discovery began when she was 14. She had a fascination for world religions and spirituality. Her sensitivity and awareness at times was challenging until she learned to strengthen her core and learn that self- care is paramount to working with people. She's always felt she has a foot in both the etheric world and the "real" world. Her report cards always had "Pam daydreams too much." Pam has been writing poetry and stories since junior high school.

She returned to the North as an adult to reclaim her roots. Training with elders in Northern Alberta and the Yukon throughout the '70s and `80's especially rounded out her perspectives. Pam is keenly interested in indigenous practices, including mysticism and shamanism, local traditional food, and medicine cultures. Pam lives in Victoria, BC with her daughter.

Chance Encounter

My cotton eyelet blouse was plastered down my back and the steamy air heavy in my lungs. The sticky heat only made Monday harder to deal with, especially when I'd spent the weekend feeling lonely and depressed. It had been over six months since Angie and I had broken up but I still couldn't seem to quit feeling sorry for myself.

My flip-flops barely made a sound as I hurried down the street, slaloming through the lunch-time shoppers, but my ankle bracelet jingled merrily against my tanned legs and my sparkly toenail polish glinted in the brilliant sunlight, matching my short fingernail manicure. I could feel the heat of the sidewalk through the soles of my bling flip-flops. I only had half an hour for lunch and an important paper deadline loomed in the back of my mind.

The restaurant was packed and noisy. Being smaller than most, I "politely" elbowed my way to the front counter to pick up my ordered take-away. A tall, burly guy shouldered past me as he was leaving and dumped me into the lap of a counter patron. He didn't even stop, probably hadn't even noticed me in the crush.

She was an island of fresh coconut in the sea of perspiration, stale cigarette smoke and food odours. I closed my eyes and breathed in the saving grace.

The only thing I could think was "Does my deodorant live up to the promises on television?"

"Oh! I'm so sorry." I exclaimed, ever the polite Canadian. Her breasts mashed into me as I grabbed for the counter. She steadied me by the elbows and I looked into her eyes.

I was, in that moment, stunned. The most fascinating, exotic green eyes sparkled back at me. They were rimmed with a fringe of the longest, blackest lashes I'd ever seen. As I stared at them, tryingto see if the lashes were real, her eyes smiled. The corner of her mouth lifted only slightly. Her hands were warm and soft, strong hands with beautifully long fingers. I imagined her gently plucking an apple (peach? Whatever.) off a tree, up on a ladder in a gypsy-style dress, her rich auburn hair cascading down her back in silky waves.

I shook my head and started to climb off her lap, but she squeezed my elbows. As she moistened her lips to speak, I caught a flash of impossibly whiteteeth. Her pink tongue peeked out for a second. "Are you sure you can stand?" she asked huskily. The voice was otherworldly ;maybe I'd actually taken that guys elbow to the head. It was as if the air had turned viscous, or my ears had suddenly filled with water.

"Um, ah," I stuttered, and slid off to stand on my own, still gazing at her face. My colour rising, I gave my head another shake. When I blushed, it clearly showed through my light tan. She laughed then and I heard angel bells tinkling.

My embarrassment deepened, but her smile was kind and she patted my arm. I couldn't guess her age. It was somewhere between 25 and a well preserved 172. She had a look of wisdom about her. I wasn't usually so inarticulate. My hand went to my throat and I wondered where my voice had fled.

She tossed back her hair, tilted her head back and laughed again. My insides went all mushy and I closed my eyes and gripped the counter. I tried to re-start my breathing, but it was difficult. My face burned and I wished I could sink through the black and white tiled floor. "Do you always have this effect on people?" I croaked.

"No," she smiled, "only on those who I am attracted to…it's a gift" she shrugged elaborately "and a curse." I wanted to put my hands on her shoulders, to feel her energy, but I curled my fists tightly and shoved them into my pockets.

Now I really didn't know what to say. I thought of myself as completely ordinary looking, pretty much average in every way: mousy brown hair as straight as sticks, plain features, okay eyes, not much in the rack department. Average build – okay a little on the short side. All in all, not something that would catch the eye of this Goddess.

Was she from here? If not, what was she doing in Victoria? How long would she be here? A million questions burned in my brain, but I couldn't speak. Luckily, I was saved from embarrassing myself.

Jorge handed over my bagged lunch and I dug out the crumpled bills in my pocket. "Here's your usual, Tina. Sorry it took so long – you can see why." His eyes swept the packed joint.

"Thanks." I smiled at him. "Keep the change." It was our usual exchange; they were the best. I glanced back at the vision sitting on the swivel stool – she looked at me expectantly, one magnificently shaped eyebrow elevated, oh so slightly. "Um, I've got to get back to work," I pointed in that general direction with my chin. It was unsatisfying, to say the least.

She nodded and turned back to her own lunch, "Safe Journey," she said. It felt like a blessing. I hesitated again then headed for the door and took a last look to find her watching me with that beguiling smile. She lifted her hand to wave almost as if in benediction.

My heart was crushing as if under a heavy weight – was I having a damn heart attack? I hurried back down the street and choked back sudden tears. The brightness of the day seemed to dim. I shifted the bulk of my lunch bag under my left arm and shoved my right hand deep into my pocket again. A corner of something caught under my nail and I yelped. I pulled out a card. "Sasha" – the name with an email emblazoned in gold leaf. My mood lifted and my heart soared! Sasha, I rolled the name around on my tongue. What a glorious day!

Peninah Rost

Peninah is a recovering teacher living in the Kootenays. Her idea of a good time is to visit a Farmer's market, soak in a hot spring or hole up in a coffee shop and tap away at her laptop, preferably all three in one day.

"Behind Ornately Carved Doors" is a deleted scene from her upcoming novel *Help Wanted*. She dabbles in detective fiction, creative non-fiction, fantasy, science fiction, poetry and pretty much anything else that will get her writing. She is still trying to find a way to successfully talk with her hands through paper.

Beyond Ornately Carved Doors

"Paul, you're looking much less gaunt these days. I guess the food I bring is being put to good use," stated Sally, assessing me with a motherly eye. Sally, the most senior witch working at Store 13 had, in a sense, adopted me. Not only had she stuck her neck out and got me, a mere human - though she hadn't known I was human at the time - the job, she had spent a goodchunk of the last year helping to keep me safe from customers and staff alike. Additionally, my sad twenty- year-old-male menu had been augmented considerably by the delicious food that came out of Sally's kitchen, though she gave the credit to someone named John. Her husband, I assumed.

"I see from the schedule that neither of us is working on Thursday evening. Would you like to comeover for dinner?"

I thought about it for a moment. A home cooked meal was a major enticement. However, I wasn't sure I really wanted to see where Sally lived. My friend fit right in to the area around the store where we both worked. It's in prime bag lady, junkie, and dumpster diver territory. Sally's hair was always pulled back in anuntidy bun with enough wisps to hide most of a pretty face, as far as I could judge. She usually dressed inwhat looked like rejects from a rummage sale held in the 1960's. Below the surface? I had no idea exceptthat she had always been kind to me. While Sally knew almost everything about me, I knew very little about her, which seemed unfair.

"I won't promise to tell you all of my secrets," said Sally, with a sly grin.

Right, don't forget she can read your mind.

Sally laughed and continued, "You can't imagine what a hassle it is sometimes. And before you ask, I was born with it. My mother thought it would be a wonderful gift. Like most parents, she was wrong at least half the time."

"Despite you reading my mind and making me nervous, I'd like to come," I said. Working at Store 13 surrounded by witches, vampires, and werewolves - not to mention a couple of dozen creatures I didn't really have a name for - had helped me to develop my innate sarcasm and an industrial-strength thick skin. Life as the only human employee of the store wasn't easy. Sally might bring me dinner but other co-workers wanted to have me FOR dinner. Also for many of them, human niceties, like personal space and table manners, were foreign concepts.

***

While Sally made sure I didn't starve, my friend Francois, a vampire with a serious fashion habit, had picked out , and purchased but that's a whole different story, the presentable half of my wardrobe. I chose exclusively from that portion when I got dressed on Thursday. Invitations to dinner had been pretty rare in my life. As the only child of drug addicts, dinner itself had been rare enough at our house. Despite the way Sally was usually dressed, I wanted to dress to impress.

As arranged, I was leaning against the wall by Sally's car. She was late but her vehicle was interesting enough to entertain me while I waited.

The broom on Sally's roof rack was only the beginning. I ran my fingers along one of the many scrapes on the side of the ancient Volvo station wagon. Each scratch seemed to reveal a different base colour. Aquamarine, bright red, purple, and lime green showed through the dark brown paint on top. The varnish had peeled off many places that were still brown making the surface look more like bark than metal. The car, which was older than I was, had more than enough space for the random collection within. She had made no attempt to hide the teetering piles of spell books that must sway back and forth with every turn. Between the stacks were clusters of bags and boxes. I'd seen those types of containers before, in the enchantment ingredients aisle. Working in a magical store had really opened my eyes.

"I hope you haven't been waiting too long," said Sally, coming up behind me.

I whipped around, startled. Sally grinned at me. My stomach churned a little. Maybe I had dressed up too much? A long yellow skirt peeked out from under a red skirt while Sally wore a blue dress on top. Add to that a green blouse and a purple cardigan, typical Sally. She smiled, I assumed she caught a glimpse of that thought.

"Um, aren't you worried someone will steal your car? This stuff is expensive." I gestured behind me.

"Forget what you know for a moment and look again."

I wasn't sure what she meant until I looked again. Sally was a witch and a lot of the spell stuff made a drug habit look cheap but suddenly the disorganized piles transformed into garbage and the car became just another rolling repository of junk, a common enough sight here in Vancouver's East Side.

"Good camouflage." It dawned on me that it wasn't even magic. People don't see what they don't want to see. Most people would have avoided even looking through the window for fear of what they might see. "But wouldn't it be easier to just store it all at home?"

"No, not really." She left it at that.

I climbed into the car, squirming as quietly as possible to find a comfortable position. My boney ass was at war with the multitude of springs.

We left downtown behind us and the car was clanking loudly through one of the swankier neighbourhoods. I gripped the door handle as the car shuddered around a corner. I wondered if the car was going to survive long enough to get us to Sally's.

First were the expensive townhouses, rubbing shoulders with boutiques and fancy restaurants. Then we passed through clusters of big houses on smallish lots. After that the houses stayed the same size but the lots grew. And still, we kept going. Finally, we were driving through a tunnel of trees and the houses were no longer visible but every once in awhile a driveway, complete with stone lions and wrought iron gates, would appear discretely between the trees.

My head was oscillating between "Where are you taking me?" and "You live around here?" I figured that at some point the road would drop out of the socioeconomic stratosphere and land us somewhere that would fit with Sally's car and clothing so I kept my mouth shut. She returned the favour though I'm sure my thoughts were quite amusing to the witch at my side. I settled back into my seat trying to calm the nerves that had made me edge forward.

But when Sally's gnarled hand flicked the indicator it was pointing between a pair of lions. The biggest I had seen on our drive. I looked more closely noticing that the 'lions' had wings.

"Gryphons," explained Sally while the iron gates swung silently inward. The gates were taller than many houses. The wrought iron had been tortured into the shape of two dragons meeting at their muzzles and claws, their silence was eerie. Gates like that should creak, or at least hum. As the car rolled through, I glanced at the gryphon closest to me. I almost screamed when it turned its head to take a look at me.

I'm sure my eyes showed nothing but white. Sally's laugh was soft and rich, completely unlike the cackle I was used to. Yes, witches do cackle.

A tap, tap from her fingernail pulled my attention to the steering wheel. Before my eyes, the wrinkled dry hands clutching it received the mother of all makeovers. The nails lengthened and metallic blue polish flowed across each surface leaving a mirror shine. The skin pulled tight over each finger while the liberal collection of age spots faded away. I considered looking at Sally's face but I was quite aware that she was laughing at me. I kept my eyes on her bargain basement clothes which were changing as I watched. The yellow, red and green skirts crawled over each other like snakes. The ribbons of colour swirled into a pattern of flowers that adorned a smooth pencil skirt. The clashing green and purple tops that Sally had beenwearing were melting before my eyes, leaving behind a tailored jacket and jade green blouse underneath. Her hair escaped from its iron gray old lady basic bun intoa smooth silver haircut that I would bet cost a mint. Finally, I forced myself to look at Sally's face. It was still Sally, I sighed with relief, just Sally with fewer wrinkles. A sly smile played over her perfectly painted pink lips.

I thought about her transformation. "So which one is the real you?"

"Now you're starting to think," she said, approvingly.

It came to my attention that the seat under me was much more comfortable. The springs had not only repaired themselves but my long legs were no longer tangled into a space smaller than carry-on luggage. The parcels and packages had transformed into file boxes and totes, all labelled carefully, while the Volvo had moved up the ranks to a brand-new, shiny, clean...Volvo station wagon. I raised an eyebrow at the newly renovated Sally.

"What can I say? I like Volvos."

It says a lot about me that the surprise of watching Sally and the car's transformation had faded completely by the time the car swung past a house that would have dwarfed the average elementary school to pull into a three car garage.

"I assume your outfit today is care of Francois or I'd have to give you a makeover. My way is faster than the vampire's but you can't take it off and it tends to fade when I'm not paying attention." She turned to face me, scanning me critically. "I could do something with your hair." There was a hint of a question in her voice.

"No thanks, Sally. I mean it, thank you for the offer but if it's OK, I'll just leave the hair as is."

Sally smiled brightly and patted my hand. She paused for a moment. New thoughts obviously overtaking the smile. Her lips pulled in tightly. She looked almost nervous. "I should warn you; my family is a little odd and I don't discuss my job at home. At all," she said, firmly.

I was a little unsure about what I would talk about otherwise. *What do I have in common with a witch and her family?*

"You'll think of something. Besides..." She paused. "Well, I know that you'll be just fine." She patted my hand again absentmindedly. "I may have forgotten to mention that I was bringing someone home for dinner."

"Sally!" We were too far out of town for me to walk back.

"Don't worry, Paul. There is always enough food." Her reassuring smile didn't quite make it to her eyes and her hands paused twice on their journey to the door handle. She was nervous enough for both of us.

The garage door led into a kitchen big enough to hold my whole apartment. The man at the stove turned at the sound of the opening door. If a male model was about to turn 50, he would pray to look like this guy.

"Sweetheart, you're home." He smiled at Sally, turned and called, "Sally's home!" through the open door.

"Hi John," my hostess said, stepping aside to reveal me behind her. "I'd like you to meet Paul. He's a good friend from work."

Noticing me for the first time, John's smile became wooden and he attempted to break bones when he shook my hand. Luckily, years of guitar playing and manual labour had given me a decent grip so I returned the favour and succeeded in making him wince. I wasn't sure why he felt the need to start some kind of pissing contest with me but I'm a guy: you challenge me, I will accept.

We were both trying to massage some feeling back into our hands when more people filed into the room. One, a stand-in for Magnum P.I., complete with Hawaiian shirt, kissed Sally on the cheek while another, a banker type, suit and shiny shoes, put a froufrou drink into her hand. "Paul, this is Simon" – Hawaiian shirt - "and that is Peter." – shiny shoes. Both joined in John's quest to break my hand. It was seriously unfair since they only had to face one opponent and now I was up to three. I was holding myown, thank goodness, though my mind was racingaround attempting to decipher the situation I suddenlyfaced. I had expected John, I had eaten enough of his meals before, but where did Simon and Peter fit into this household?

Sally asked Peter to get me a drink and I declined for fear that he would think poison would make a suitable mixer. They were not happy to see me for some unknown reason. Showing up with an unannounced random work friend might fit into the category of annoying if you're planning a quiet eveningwith your other half, but it shouldn't cause this kind ofanimosity. Sally had said that her family was odd. Considering my upbringing, I was no stranger to odd.I just kept my customer service smile firmly in place.

The living room overlooked a terrace with a pool and a wide expanse of lawn. I sank into one of the small car- sized sofas, which practically wrapped itself around me. The room felt rich. Wooden panelling stretched from the thick carpet to the mouldings that appeared to have been borrowed from city hall or the court house. Paintings hung on the walls, not posters. It was all very different from the one grey-walled room I called home.

"So how do you know our Sally?" asked Peter, sharply.

"Paul and I work together at the Foundation." This was the first I had heard of it. Obviously, Sally took not talking about her job seriously.

"And what do you do for the Foundation?" asked John, placing a tray of fancy little bites on the coffee table. Who does appetizers for a Thursday night dinner? They hadn't known I was coming so it was obviously a normal thing around here.

I hoped Sally would field that question as well since the "Foundation" was a figment of her imagination. *Do they really not know where Sally worked?* I looked at her but she just smiled. I got the feeling that she was enjoying all this. It would be so easy to get it wrong. *What did every business need?* My clothes moved me out of the mail room and out of the janitorial staff but my age kept me out of the good generic titles like consultant and manager. A revelation came to me. "I'm an assistant." I left it at that.

"And what does that entail?" queried Simon.

"I assist, Simon." I had had enough of their prying.

"Yes, Paul is very helpful. He's also a musician, Simon." I watched as she locked eyes with Simon. His brows pulled tight for a moment as he looked at the other men and then a chagrined smile appeared on his face. He leaned over to whisper something to John who looked down, almost ashamed, and then nodded.

Whatever was going on, I was just glad she remembered. I sometimes forgot myself, Store 13 had absorbed so much of my life. I was about to mention my last gig. Well, open mike night is almost a gig.

"Simon is in the philharmonic," Sally added. "He's a wonderful trumpet player."

"Wow," I muttered, suddenly feeling a lot smaller. "I just play the guitar a little. I mostly taught myself so I'm probably not very good."

To my surprise, Simon gave me a real smile. "We all have to start somewhere. When I met Sally, I was playing the trumpet on Robson Street."

My eyes widened. It was a long way from busking downtown to playing in the Philharmonic. "I tried to busk down there but it seems that some people are a bit territorial. Or maybe I wasn't good enough?"

"Most likely you were better. That's what makes them nervous," said John, laughing. He passed a plate to Peter and mouthed something that I couldn't decipher. "Simon says that being asked who their favourite musician is annoys musicians but it seems a logical way to find out more about them. What do you think?"

"I don't mind the question but I find most people aren't prepared for the answer. It usually takes at least twenty minutes," I said, happy to feel the tension fade.

"I'm not sure the canapes will last that long," commented Peter, leaning over to offer me a plate of tiny pastries. "As long as you include some Jazz, I won't complain."

Reeling a little at the change in atmosphere, I guess Sally's look at Simon had started a chain reaction that brought me out of the dog house. "Well, the 1920 recording of *Singin' the Blues* is on my morning playlist. Plus a bunch of Billie Holiday."

"I wouldn't have thought you were old enough to be into the Blues," said Peter.

"Come on, Peter! I started listening to Louis Armstrong and Duke Ellington when I was 12," quipped Simon. "The guy knows good music when he hears it, that's all."

Our conversation centred around music, thankfully. When I was growing up, libraries were my main source of warmth and clean bathrooms. Even before I could read, I figured out the CD players that they had wired to the wall and listened to everything in the place. I learned early that people don't bug you if you are quiet and have headphones on. That and never go to the same library, soup kitchen, community centre, support group, or church too often. Music filled my world with colours that were uncommon in the rest of my life. As soon as I could read, I absorbed the music section. I even enrolled myself in every music class that the money I stole from my mother and her drugged out friends could afford. These guys were smart and when the conversation drifted on to history and its impact on art, I just sat back and listened. I realized that my reading might have been a little narrow.

Sally and Peter were arguing happily about the effect of the Norman conquest on weaving on both sides of the English Channel when a new arrival walked into the room. His straight back, confident smile and firm step announced him as, at least in his own head, cock of the walk, alpha wolf, etc.

"Charles!" Sally rose to greet him, eagerly. He wrapped his arms around her and involved her in a very passionate kiss. Not wanting to watch, I glanced around the room. The rest of their audience had drifted onto other topics of conversation, apparently oblivious.

"Paul, I'd like you to meet my husband, Charles. Charles, Paul is a friend from work."

If the reaction the others had given me was icy, Charles's reaction was Antarctic ... in the winter ... on a cold day ... with wind chill. He looked at my outstretched hand like it was a snake or possibly something that had been dead for a few weeks. He didn't shake it. I got a bare nod of welcome accompanied by narrowed eyes. He was probably memorizing my face so he could find and kill me later. Again, I was stumped for a reason.

I glanced around the room hoping for a little moral support but everyone was absorbed in their drinks and conversations though I was pretty sure they had stopped breathing when Charles entered. John looked up and gave me a thin smile and suggested we head in for dinner. Ignoring her husband's daggers, Sally took my arm, leading me into the dining room which seemed to have dropped off the set of a soap opera. I was aware that the men had paused in the living room.

"This house has been in my family for five generations," explained Sally. "We've added to it but I remember my grandmother presiding over Thanksgiving dinner at this table. She was quite the lady."

"If she was anything like her granddaughter, she must have been."

"Oh Paul!" she giggled.

"I'm not kidding, Sally. I know you don't talk about work but...if you live in a place like this, why do you work at Store 13?"

"The first time I met you, I said, 'I shop the sales.' I meant it. My ... abilities, some of them anyway, require expensive and hard to find ingredients. Store 13 is a witch's fantasy." A cloud crossed Sally's face. "You'll learn that Store 13 is a haven. Humans aren't the only ones who fight over differences and ostracize those who don't fit in. Besides I enjoy my work," said Sally, her smile returning.

I didn't want Sally to be sad so I just filed her comments for later. "You are kidding, right? You like dealing with cranky, rude and strange people?" In the previous week, I had an ogre and ogress who were very unhappy with our return policy and when an ogre gets unhappy everyone hears about it. I had also had to hide a werewolf who was in the middle of changing from a group of Japanese tourists that had wandered into the store; do you know how big a werewolf is? Not an easy thing to hide. Oh yes and one of our human customers threw up all over a display of clocks. It had been a typical week.

"Don't forget all the nice, friendly, and interesting people we deal with. Something you need to learn is the ability to enjoy life, whatever you're doing," said Sally.

"Something our Sally is very good at," added Charles, suddenly joining us. He kissed Sally's hand elaborately before taking a seat beside her. There was sadness on his handsome face. Simon and Peter clapped him on the shoulder on the way to their seats. John followed with a platter of ... hell if I knew then or even now what they were ... to me, they looked like baby lobsters. He swished in and out several times until the table was groaning.

The meal was much more pleasant than I had anticipated. I guessed that a powwow had been held and a decision made to play nice. Anyway, the gentlemen were all focused on Sally. She kept the conversation on safe topics including regaling us with a full description of her daughter Sunrise's recent travels in Europe. Though I noticed that Charles didn'thave much to say, his eyes only left Sally's face tolinger on the plate of food that he toyed with but didn't eat. Sally seemed not to notice though her eyes flicked towards the door several times, which made mewonder if someone else was going to join us.

Drawing my thoughts back to the table, John pointed out a painting of Sunrise that hung just above Sally's head. "Peter painted that last time she was home."

"It's really good. You are very talented," I said.

"Thank you but Sunrise is easy to make look beautiful." If the picture was true to life, Sunrise was very pretty. "By the way, I've come across a little house I think Sunrise would love," said Peter.

"Peter is a real estate agent," explained Sally. "Peter, you haven't bought it, have you?" Peter refused to answer though he exchanged a look with John and Simon. The witch seemed exasperated. "You boys, Sunrise isn't likely to settle down any time soon, sadly." I wondered with a bit of a chill if these guys were involved with Sally's daughter. They looked too old, the portrait on the wall put her close to my age,but I wasn't taking anything for granted. The conversation drifted on to food and from there towine. I listened in awe as my dinner companions talked about far-off places that I hadn't even dreamt of visiting. It turned out dinner was Vietnamese and the wine was Argentinian. All I knew was that it was all delicious.

Once we finished eating, Sally lead the way back into the living room where she and I sprawled on the couches and chatted about this and that. The men hadn't joined us; I had no complaints about that. I tried to ask about our dinner companions but Sally justgave me lists of their achievements and nothing about her relationship with them. The call of nature dragged me to my feet and following Sally's detailed instructions I found the bathroom.

On my way back, I heard voices coming from the dining room and my curiosity got the better of me.

"Come, come, Charles, you had to know this was going to happen at some point. It happens to all of us in the end," came Peter's voice.

"But so soon?" said Charles, his voice sounded muffled. I realized that it was clogged with tears. I was horrified but not horrified enough to stop listening.

"My question is: how will he fit in?" added John.

"He's rather young," commented Simon.

"He's younger than Sunrise!" moaned Charles, desperation in his tone. "You should never have allowed Sally to go off to work at that Foundation."

"Do you seriously think I could have stopped her?" chuckled Simon. "Peter, you met her at the Foundation, didn't you?"

"Yes, I think so. I remember meeting her so clearly, the rest was unimportant, just background," he responded in a dreamy voice.

"The reality is that if things go that direction..." started Simon.

"What do you mean if? Sally brought him home for dinner; you all know what that means!" Charles cried out. There was a brief pause.

"I remember the first time Sally brought you here for dinner, Charles," stated Peter. There was a trace of sadness in his voice too.

"If things go that direction," Simon repeated, firmly, "and I truly believe it is just an 'if', it's up to us to make sure he finds a place here. Though we may have to build an addition ... again."

I was thoroughly confused. What on earth were they talking about? Sally invited me over for dinner notto move in.

"Do you usually eavesdrop on private conversations, whoever you are?" whispered a voice inmy ear.

I almost swallowed my tongue.

"Come on," laughed a young woman quietly, dragging me away from the door. I recognized her instantly from her portrait in the dinning room. It was Sally's daughter, Sunrise. I still hadn't recovered my ability to speak when she pulled me into the living room.

Sally was rising gracefully from the couch as we walked in. "Sunrise. I expected you an hour ago." She gave no indication of shock though the discussion at the dinner table suggested that Sunrise wasn't expected home for several weeks. She wrapped her arms around her daughter in a giant hug.

Extricating herself from her mother's embrace, Sunrise chuckled. "One day I would like to surprise you."

"It's never going to happen, child. I will always be a witch. That comes with certain benefits." Sally laughed.

"Actually, Mum, I believe you must be slipping. The Husbands think you're eyeing up this youngster as your next husband. I would have thought you would have picked that up, I doubt they are thinking of anything else!"

I stopped breathing. I resented the 'youngster' comment but did they really think that Sally had designs on me? Did she?

"I must be slipping. My lord, those boys haven't got the brains the goddesses gave a haystack!" hooted

Sally. "Sunrise, this is Paul. He's the young man from the store I spoke to you about. Don't worry, Paul, my daughter knows all about my job and what I am."

As if I was concerned about that. I don't know about the 'boys' but my brain was starting to ache. Its capacity was being sorely taxed. I was still confused and pretty concerned too.

"Just wait here for a moment, I'd better set things straight," said Sally, stopping only to hug Sunrise again. "Please keep Paul company for a moment."

"Um, say thanks to John, and all of them for me," I stuttered, nervously. Maybe Sally did have ulterior motives in inviting me here, she was a witch after all and I knew next to nothing about witches. Perhaps, I would end up as one of the Husbands, as Sunrise put it, whatever that meant.

"I'll do that and, Paul, I have no designs on you. Stop worrying, you were invited here for a meal, not a lifetime," said Sally, reminding me once again that she could read my mind.

Relieved but still confused, I stared off into space, trying desperately to shake the various clippings of information that I had into an order that made some kind of sense. I didn't know what to say to Sunrise and she was still chuckling to herself, at my expense, I was sure. Suave with women, I'm not.

She must have decided to take pity on me. "My mother has been married five times and all of them live in this house. She's not some kind of evil witch. They stay because they want to. Believe me, she has tried to shake them loose."

"They're all her ex's?" I said.

"Charles is her current husband. I can't say it was always easy growing up in this house. True, there was never any problem with finding chaperones for school trips and I wasn't a latch-key kid. John was the first and he makes a brilliant homemaker."

"Is he your father?" I asked.

"No," Sunrise's pleasant voice tightened with anger.

"I'm sorry," I said.

Sunrise smiled again. "It's not you. That was a very different situation. He wasn't human. It's a bit hard to explain and the explanation isn't something I like to think about." My dinner twisted around in my gut; the baby lobsters were dancing to the tune of 'What the hell was he?!'

"Relax, Paul. And I promise my mother has no intention of adding you to our happy family, though I'm pretty sure you will always be welcome as a guest."

"He certainly is," said Charles from the doorway, his face sporting an incandescent level of smile, his arm securely around Sally's slim waist. The rest of the Husbands flowed into the room, adding their agreement.

"Thank you all very much," I said, glad to no longer be public enemy number one. "John, dinner was amazing."

"I'm glad you liked it." John grinned and brought a large carrier bag out from behind his back. "Leftovers," he said, handing me the bag.

"Paul, if you want to come hear some classical music sometime, you would be welcome to come to the philharmonic. Let Sally know and I'll get you tickets," said Simon.

"I better get you home," said Sally, smiling. Her look was more mothering than any I had ever experienced. I'll admit I was kind of enjoying her urge to adopt me. All the same, it was time to change the subject before she spit dabbed a smudge on my cheek.

"Mum, why don't I drive him home?" interjected Sunrise. "If I can borrow a car, mine's still under the dust cover, I assume?" She left the question hanging.

"You can borrow mine, sweetheart," said Peter, tossing her a set of keys. Sally protested that Sunrise must be tired but Sunrise insisted. I guessed that I wasn't the only one who had seen the look of relief on Charles's face as soon as the offer was made.

"Besides the rest of you have drunk five bottles of wine according to the kitchen counter," said Sunrise with a grin.

I felt like I was in the receiving line at a wedding as I shook each of their hands as I was ushered out. No one tried to break my hand this around. Sally hugged me as strongly as I had seen her hug her daughter.

We ended up in a very nice Mercedes that had been parked behind the house. The driveway swung past the front of the house. I glanced back to see Sally and Charles, flanked by the rest of the household, framed by the light spilling out through the open door.

"I had hoped it would be Simon who ponied up with the keys. He's got a wicked little Porsche. Ohwell, beggars can't be choosers," said Sunrise.

"Do they even know that your mother's a witch?"

"They haven't got a clue," she said with a chuckle. "They just think they are impressively bohemian in their attitudes. Granted, I'm pretty damn sure theydon't tell their friends and coworkers how ourhousehold works but it does work. They're happy and in this world, you can't ask for better than that."

"Does she have a spell on them?"

"A couple of dozen at least. But I swear their delusion and devotion are entirely self-inflicted. Like most people's."

"After everything I've seen at store 13, I believe it. I wonder why your mother wanted me to meet your family," I said.

"Knowing my mother, she probably wanted you to meet me."

Oh great, I thought, as the confusion took hold again, bringing its friend embarrassment along for the ride. Despite the darkness, I was sure Sunrise could see the blush that covered me from head to foot. This was going to be a long ride home, I thought, as Sunrise laughed.

Ron Kearse

Ron has led a nomadic life having lived in most provinces in Canada. His resumé is varied andcolourful as he's worked at everything from a tree farm in northern Ontario, assisted with special projects for a major resource company in Alberta, and worked with Aboriginal offenders in the federal penal system in British Columbia.

Author, columnist, blogger, photographer and broadcaster, Ron has published two novels: *Road Without End* and *Just Outside of Hope* along with a book of his photographs called *Lost History*.

Ron's future plans include travelling throughout the world writing, filming and taking photos. He's presently writing his third novel which he hopes to have published in the spring of 2015. He lives with his partner Steven Foster in East Vancouver.

The Snow Falls on Montreal

"Prochaine station, Berri-UQAM," announces the robotic female voice over the P.A. system as the Métro slows to a halt inside a cavernous hall. The doors slide open as people quickly move outside while being jostled by those wanting inside of the car. The noise level immediately rises as six children board the train with three adults. The children chatter excitedly as the adults smile and look on. A couple of the children remind me of my son and daughter when they were kids.

I stare out the window taking in as much of the activity as I can in the moments that we're stopped here. A large screen hypnotically flashes various images at the waiting crowds on the platforms:advertisements, news headlines, weather forecasts, sports highlights and even the top ten music countdown in North America.

A short, older Muslim woman enters the train carrying two huge shopping bags. She wears a long, grey overcoat and a brightly coloured hijab swaddles her neck and head. A young man immediately jumps up and offers her his seat. She smiles and says, "Merci," as she sits down. The young man smiles back and nods. Then I hear that familiar high pitched squeal indicating the doors are about to slide shut. The train moves on to the next stop.

"Prochaine station, Beaudry," announces the robotic voice once more. I join a handful of others as we make our way to the nearest exit. The train slows to a stop and the doors slide open. I leave the Métro and exit the station on to Rue Ste. Catherine.

Heavy snowflakes are falling, covering everything with a gentle blanket. I love this city, preferring its live-and-let-live charm to the hard-nosed business attitude of Toronto, the place I grew up, the place I call home. So anytime there is a chance to go on a business trip here I take it.

I walk down the street to the Second Cup Coffee Shop in the gay village and order. The young woman smiles pleasantly as I pay her. I take my coffee to a seat by the window so I can people watch.

In this quiet moment I reflect on my life and how it has changed over the past couple of years. I got divorced three years ago because I could no longer hide the fact that I prefer men to women. My former wife is now seeing another guy, my kids have both finished college and one has recently married.

I never thought it would come to this. Having kidded myself all these years that I was straight, I followed all the rules—you know, got married, had kids, got a secure job, a mortgage and all was to befine. But reality doesn't work like that. I couldn't fight who I really am. I'd long to be with guys and yes, clandestinely I sought other men for those few moments of pleasure I could get, feeling their naked bodies against mine. So here I am, in my late-50's, thinning on top and getting thicker around the middle, the red beard I had sported for many years is entirely silver…and now I'm alone.

Raising the cup to my mouth, my eyes connect with the most beautiful pair of green eyes I've ever seen. They are looking at me through the window of the shop, smiling and piercing my very being. I refocus. I'm immobilized. He's a man seemingly about my age, thin with a graying goatee and wearing a black tuque. I slowly lower my cup as our eyes lock on each other. At this moment everything is happening in slow motion. His face is radiant as he smiles at me so I smile back. He winks and quickly disappears.

I jump out of my chair, startling customers around me, and stride hastily to the door to see where he's gone. I look down the street and don't see any sign of him—he's disappeared into the crowd. So I return to my table, down my coffee and walk back to my hotel room to finish some of my day's work all the while thinking, *who was he?*

***

I'm looking through the selection of DVD's at *Archambeault Music* after work. Two days have passed since that guy looked in through the window at me and I've still not been able to get him out of my head. I had given up all hope of anybody giving me a glance, so now when this stranger shows an interest, it's affecting me.

I can't believe this. That fellow with the yellow scarf in the next aisle. It's him. At least I think it's him! I can only see his profile so it's hard for me to tell. He's wearing that black tuque on his head and he's holding a CD box set. He looks at it, puts it back in the rack, checks his watch and turns to leave. I watch him as he walks up the aisle, and just when he's about to disappear into the crowd he turns and looks directly at me, points, smiles and winks before going out the door. I stand there momentarily, and then I hastily squeeze my way through the crowd to get outside.

Squinting through the blowing snow I look across the street to the Berri-UQAM Métro station—nothing. So I look east down the crowded sidewalk hoping to see that yellow scarf—nothing. I look west up Rue Ste. Catherine—nothing. Damn! I walk eastward toward the gay village and vow that if he turns up again I'm going to find out who he is.

I keep a lookout for him while walking and go into that same coffee shop where I first saw him. I get my coffee and sit at an empty table near the back of the shop. That's when this same man, coffee cup in hand, appears out of nowhere, brazenly pulls out a chair and joins me at the table.

"Bonsoir," he smiles.

"B-b-bonsoir," I respond awkwardly.

"Ah, you are English."

"Do I speak French with an English accent?"

"Yes, of course," he grins. "J'm'appelle Marc Beauchesne," he winks and smiles.

"I'm Peter, Peter Collard."

"Pleasure to meet you Pierre Collard," he raises his coffee cup to me and I return the gesture.

"The pleasure is mine," I answer and we watch each other as we both have a sip.

"So," I begin, "do you usually just sit down with strangers to talk?"

"Only if I want to know them," he says. "That is something you would not do?"

I don't know what to say.

"You must be from Toronto," he laughs.

"It's *that* obvious?" I smile.

He nods his head while laughing. "People from Toronto are so, how you say, *stifled.*"

"Stifled?"

"Yes. Toronto people have trouble with their feelings…"

"Well, I don't know about…"

"You know all about the stock market, but you stop yourselves from expressing who you are. Like it is some big secret."

There's a moment of silence.

"That's okay," he smiles and winks, "I like what I see."

"Well," I say, "for a long time my life *was* a big secret."

"A-ha," he says, "You are divorced and have a couple of grown kids?"

I can't believe what I'm hearing.

"Your mouth is open," he says.

"Am I made of glass? How did you know that?"

"You wear your history well," he answers.

I'm embarrassed, I never realized I wore my life on my sleeve in such a way.

"No need to be embarrassed," he says as he gently touches my hand, "that is a common story for men our age."

I don't know what to make of this guy. Is he genuine or is this some kind of a game he's playing? Inspite of my doubts about him I say, "I haven't been able to get you out of my mind since I saw you the other evening."

"Good," he smiles. "You know what?"

"What?"

"I am hungry, do you want to go for something to eat?"

"I have some leftovers from last night in the fridge back in my hotel room, I was just going to…"

"Bon, c'mon with me then," he interrupts, "I know a good bistro."

"But…"

Marc is already up and heading for the door. He turns back to me and motions me to hurry. So I grab my things and hasten to catch up with him. I'm shocked when he grabs my hand as we walk down the street. I snatch my hand back as if I'd just burned it on a stove, he stops and looks at me.

"This is Montréal Pierre. People do not care if we are holding hands in public."

"But we've just met and…"

"…Yes, and it is good to finally meet you."

He takes my hand in his once more.

"See," he smiles again, "nobody has taken their guns to us."

I say nothing. We take the Métro up to Le Plateau and walk over to a little bistro called *Le Flambard* at the corner of Rachel and Rue Ste. Christophe. It's a charming place where Marc and I spend the next two hours. Then we decide to walk back down to the gay village and to my hotel room. I invite him up and he stays the night with me.

***

When I haven't been working, I've been spending time with Marc. It's hard to put into words how I feel when I'm around him. *Alive*, would be a good word to describe it. It's been too long since I've felt this way about anybody. He's so animated and spontaneousthat being around him is a pleasurable contrast to my predictable and well-scheduled life in Toronto. This is what I've been thinking as we're walking through the gay village holding hands.

"What is on your mind, Pierre?"

"Marc, I could live this way forever."

"What way, Pierre?"

"Well, you know, I wish I didn't have to go back to Toronto and my predictable life."

"You do not have to if you do not want to, Pierre."

"You're right, I don't *have* to…"

"So since you know you do not *have* to, means you *want* to?"

"Well, no…"

"So what is stopping you?"

"I've got responsibilities and…"

"Pierre, you can walk away from those résponsibilités anytime you want. What is reallystopping you?"

I hesitate.

"That answer will do, Pierre," Marc says breaking my train of thought.

"I don't have an answer, Marc."

"What do you have to lose by leaving Toronto? If you really do not want your old way of life why not change it? Why live the boring life you have beentelling me you are so tired of living?

"I have a good life in Toronto, Marc."

Marc stops, looks directly into my eyes and says, "Why live a *good* life when you can have a *fantastic* life with me?"

"But Marc, we barely know each other."

"Do you not know yourself?"

"Well, yes."

"Good, we can explore each other together!"

"But I can't just up and leave."

"Have you never acted on, how you say in English, your guts?"

"That has its place but it's not a logical thing to do. You can't plan and strategize when you think things like that."

"Ah, you are so Toronto! No wonder you are so stifled! Get that idea out of your head! Life is not about planning and working until you are dead! In Québec we say, *Vous ne pouvez pas travailler toute votre vie, il faut vivre!* You cannot work all your life, you have to live!"

I hesitate once more, "Well…"

"Well, what, Pierre? Why do you resist? Why not seize life by the balls before it does that to you? You act like your life is over but you are still a youngspirit—like me. We are only middle aged and still have a lot of fun to do," he says as he turns to me and flashes that sweet smile of his. I look at him and I can'tcontain myself. I kiss him on the lips, right there, on the sidewalk, in front of all who pass by. Even as I'm doing it I can't *believe* I'm doing it. It's not like me to do something spontaneous like this. But during this moment I don't care. His face lights up.

"*That* is more like it," he smiles. "you are learning well."

I smile.

"To be truly alive you have to live the way each moment tells you. Like you did right now." Then he puts his arms around me and deeply kisses me.

"C'mon let's go," Marc says.

"Where?"

"Up to Mount Royal. You should see the city at night, spectaculaire!"

That sounds like fun to me, so we walk to the Papineau Métro Station. From there we take the Métro to Station Guy de Maissoneuve, we switch to a couple of buses to find ourselves on Chemin Remembrance at the top of Mount Royal. We disembark at a hugetraffic circle and, hand-in-hand, I follow Marc as he leads me down a narrow and well-lit road into the woods. We follow the road until we reach anescarpment and there, laid out like a beautiful carpet of light before us, is downtown Montreal. We put our arms around each others shoulders and gaze silently at the splendid scene. It's perfect.

Later, as we're walking back through the woods to the traffic circle, he catches me off guard as he tackles me into a snow bank and we roll around laughing and kissing each other like a pair of teenagers. Then he stops and looks at me.

"What?" I ask.

He has a sly smile.

"What?" I repeat.

"Let's make love."

"What?"

"Let's make love."

"Here? Now?"

"Oui. You afraid?"

"Well, what if someone sees us?"

"Then they will probably watch," he says as he undoes his coat and lays it on top of the snow beside us. Then he removes his sweater and t-shirt. He stops, looks at me and says, "C'mon, take off your clothes." He keeps his black tuque on which makes him look especially sexy as he undresses.

I look around to see if we're alone, and hesitantly take off my jacket, lay it on the snow beside his, then my sweater, shirt, and before I know it, here we are. The two of us laying naked on top of our jackets in a hot embrace deeply kissing each other. It's cold, it's brisk and we're naked on a snow bank making love. How Canadian is this?

***

Unbeknownst to me, Marc phoned a local rental company while I was in the shower and rented a car for today, "I want to take you for a drive to see the pretty little villages outside of Montréal," he said. "You can still see old stone homes and churches from the 18th and 19th centuries." So Marc and I had breakfast and now we are off on a beautiful sunny winter's day.

We drive across the Jacques Cartier Bridge through Longueuil and east to Boucherville. We arrive at the main church just as mass is ending. I had forgotten that it's Palm Sunday and I'm surprised that in order to receive a palm you must donate $2.00. When I was a young boy going to Catholic school palms were just given to each member of the congregation. "Ah," Marc says, "but in those days the church was still rich, it is not rich anymore." Good point.

After we finish exploring we drive over the Richeleau River where we explore the village of St. Marc.

"Am I going to have to call *you* St. Marc now?" I tease him.

"Now you are being a cock to me, Pierre," he kids.

"I think you mean, prick."

We laugh as we pull into a small restaurant overlooking the river where we have a really goodpizza for lunch then we carry on to another village called St. Antoine. By the time we're through exploring St. Antoine it's mid-afternoon and time to head backto Montréal.

On our way back we stop at a village called Varrenes and visit a co-op gallery where local artistsare selling their works for excellent prices! I buy Marc a small painting for $50.00 that I see him admiring. Just seeing him smile as I give it to him, makes me feel that I could spend every moment of every day with him.

We walk to a nearby park on the waterfront where we watch a team of men practicing rescuing people who have fallen through the ice. All of the rescuepersonnel are clad head to toe in orange insulated suitsand I find it interesting to watch how they maneuver along the ice to conduct a rescue mission.

"I think it's time to go back home, Pierre. I want to make you dinner tonight."

"If that's what you want to do then let's go," I say.

***

Tonight we've been relaxing and Marc is cooking a chicken and making *patat frites*. I come up behind him while he's working at the sink and put my arms around him. I kiss the back of his neck and say, "I could live this way forever."

"You keep telling me that, Pierre," he says as he turns to look at me. "I would love for you to stay with me. I feel so, how do you say, *comfortable* with you."

"I feel the same about you Marc."

"You say you want to live this way forever, then do it. For you, for me, for us! I ask again, what do you have to lose, Pierre?"

I look into his eyes and his words take hold of me like nobody's ever have. I hold him and kiss him. We look at each other silently and I kiss him again.

I take a deep breath and say, "I'm staying."

"You took a deep sigh to say that?"

"And it came right from my heart."

A smile draws across Marc's face. "You will not regret this Pierre. We will have so much fun together." We kiss deeply then Marc suddenly pushes me back, "Tabarnak! I cannot let le patat frites burn!"

***

Who was I kidding? I'm thinking this as I hurriedly pack my things into my suitcase. I'm going back to Toronto; don't know when I'll be back and my train leaves in less than an hour so I'm panicking. I hate good byes and having spent this time with Marc has made me feel so alive again that I can't bear the thought of it ending. But at the same time I can't afford to be living daydreams. Where was my head? What was I thinking that I could just toss my career aside to be with Marc and everything would be all right? That was totally irresponsible of me. I spent last night back here at the hotel to finish up the project forwork and then I didn't sleep very well thinking about this.

I want so much to toss in the job, but thinking about it long and hard, I know it would be reckless of me to do that so suddenly. Where would the stability in my life be? I need stability and security. I'm not some thirty-something guy anymore I'm supposed to know better. I can feel my pulse racing as I hurry to be on time for the train.

Marc and I had set a date about an hour ago just to have a coffee and spend the afternoon together but I left a message on his phone to say couldn't go because I was going back after all. I fought with myself over that decision. I'm going to miss him but his warmth, sincerity and affection are what I will miss the most. I haven't met anybody in Toronto who even comes close to Marc as somebody I could see spending the rest of my time with. I would love to have all of that but I have responsibilities and they have to be met.

I finish putting the last of my things in the suitcase and zip it up when there's a knock on the door. I open it to see Marc standing there looking worried.

"Marc!"

"What has happened, Pierre? Why have you changed your mind?"

He stops short as he sees my suitcase lying on the bed packed and ready to go.

"Oh," he says, "you are really leaving."

"Please listen, Marc…"

"You were going to leave me without even saying good bye to my face?"

"I need to explain…"

"No, no need to explain, Pierre. I see you've made up your mind about us."

"I would love to stay here with you Marc but I have a lot of responsibilities in Toronto and…"

"…and they come before you and your happiness." I'm taken aback.

"Have you not had any fun here with me, Pierre?"

"I've had more fun with you than I've had in the last ten years!"

He shrugs his shoulders and motions toward my suitcase, "So why are you going? We had a date and you did not show up. We were going to spend the afternoon together. You would not even tell me why you are leaving? Do you not even like me *that* much?"

"Please, let me explain…"

"There is no explanation Pierre. This all speaks to me very loud."

"Marc, I was afraid…"

"Of what?"

"This whole situation with you.…"

"What is so frightening about it?"

"Well…"

"Tell me, what is it?"

"I'm…I'm afraid that I'm having feelings for you. I'm afraid that I, I might even be falling in love with you."

"And that is so bad that you are going to run away from me like a coward?"

"No Marc, I…"

"Do you really prefer your life in Toronto than being here with me?"

"No, I like being here with you."

"But you've chosen to go back to Toronto and you weren't even going to tell me to my face. Is that the way you express feelings of love?"

"Marc, please…"

"Say nothing more, Pierre. This speaks very loudly to me. I am very hurt. I thought we were having a good time together. I thought you said you were staying with me."

"Marc, this was a last minute decision…"

"I do not understand you, Pierre!" he raises his voice. "You tell me one thing and then you do the opposite. What are you about? Is this a game you like to play with people? J'men calice tu responsibilités! Who do you think you are playing head fucks with me like that? Do you think I am a child who does not know anything?"

"No Marc, you aren't."

"Oui! I am not! Fuck you, Pierre Collard!" he says as he walks out of the room door slamming it behind him.

I feel something leave me. The panic and worry about getting the train on time are gone but so is that aliveness I felt while I was with him. The room is silent and I start shaking. What have I done? Once again I'm alone. *Congratulations, Peter*, I think, *you've screwed yourself royally again.* I don't know whether I want to scream in anger or cry.

***

The line for the train to Toronto is long as usual. I stare at the ground knowing full well that I've lost something precious in Marc. All I feel is this large, empty space inside me. But most of all I see Marc's face and hear his voice egging me on and having…fun. The emptiness I'm feeling is made even more painful by the knowledge that I chose to go back to Toronto and made my decision out of fear of change ratherthan embracing it, and Marc's affection.

I'm feeling something else inside of me, something that's growing like a bubble about to burst. I don't know what it is, all I know is I have to do something, anything to get back with Marc…somehow. A conductor appears at the small gate that leads downstairs to the trains, unlocks and opens it. The line begins moving forward as he takes boarding passes and I can't take this anymore.

I quickly take out my smart phone almost dropping it and find Marc's number; I've just got to speak to him one more time. I'm hoping beyond hope that he'll find it in his heart to forgive me, but I won't blame him if he doesn't. His line is ringing.

"Bonjour, c'est Marc."

"Marc, it's Peter," I stop as I talk. "Please don't hang up. I can't take this any more. I need you, Marc. I can't go back to Toronto, not after being with you. I'm so sorry I did what I did and I'm hoping that you'll somehow forgive me. I'll do anything you want, anything for your forgiveness and, and I'm hoping you'll give me a second chance."

There's silence on the other end.

"Marc? Are you still there?"

"Oui."

"Please say something to me?"

"How do I know you mean this, Pierre?"

I'm silent.

"I cannot hear you, Pierre."

"I know it would be hard for you to trust me after that Marc but I'm willing to do whatever it takes to win that trust back."

"Do you not have résponsibilités in Toronto? Are they not more important than you and me?"

"Fuck the responsibilities, Marc. They aren't important anymore. *We* are! *Our* lives! You and me!"

The line moves further ahead and now I'm in panic mode again because there's silence on the other end of the line. "Marc. Are you there? Marc, please answer."

"I am here," he says as he takes the phone from me and turns it off. "Marc, what…? How?"

He has a serious look on his face, "Do you think I would just let you run away from me like that without a fight?"

"Do you guys mind turning off this soap opera so we can get on the train?" says a large man in a business suit behind us.

The two of us look around to see the widened gap in the line between the people going through the gate and us.

Marc grabs my suitcase and takes it out of the line, "Je suis désolé," he says to the people behind us. The gap in the line quickly closes as people continue to board the train. Then he turns his attention to me still sporting that serious look on his face.

"And as for you," he says, "I am willing to give you another chance, but do not do me like that again or I will send you back to Toronto myself. Tucomprends?"

I slowly nod my head like an errant boy being punished by his teacher. He kisses me and I look into his hypnotic green eyes. I'm silent.

"I am so, so sorry I did that to you, Marc."

"Good," he says and rests his head on my chest. I hold him tight and kiss the top of his head.

"The train can go without me. I want to stay here."

"Are you *sure* that is what you want, Pierre."

"Yes."

"Good. Now, we are going back to my house so I can pack."

"Where are you going?"

"With you back to Toronto to help you pack so you come back here with me."

"Why do you want to do that?"

"So I can make sure you do not change your mind again."

I laugh out loud as he takes my hand and leads me to the street outside the station to get one of the cabs waiting at the entrance. I breathe in the brisk winter air. *A new life in a new town* I think as I look around me while the snow falls on Montréal.

Glossary of French Terms:

- Prochaine station: The next station
- Métro: subway
- J'm'appelle Marc Beauchesne: My name is Marc Beauchesne
- Chemin: roadway, path, alley
- spectaculaire! Spectacular!
- Vous ne pouvez pas travailler toute votre vie, il faut vivre!: You cannot work all your life, you have to live!
- Tabarnak!: Commonly used as a swear word in French Canadian slang.
- Patat Frites: Fried Potatoes (French Fries)
- J'men calice tu responsibilités: (loosely translated) – I don't give a f*ck about your responsibilities!
- "Bonjour, c'est Marc." Hello, this is Marc.
- Je suis désolé: I'm sorry
- Tu comprends?: Do you understand?

S.M. King

I was born.

I'm not dead. Yet.

Not quite, but that could change at any moment. (Stay away from me with that mallet, you Monty Python lover, you!)

I'm heavily overweight, radically underpaid, massively overworked, and strangely at ease.

My favourite saying is: "In face of the age of the universe, all this means NOTHING. It's an incredibly liberating adage. It allows me to put aside false notions of relevancy and misplaced urges to leave a legacy, and simply enjoy every breath and every smile.

If you're clever (and you know you are), you now know more about my inner character than any of the folks with whom I've worked for the last 40 years.

Once again, Thanks to A.B. King for his kind assistance in editing this and his awesome insights into things Universal. Every girl should have a brother like him.

Vide Cor Meum

She fled.

She fled into the hills. Above the river settlements, deep into jungle, she ran. Heart pounding, seeking refuge.

She fled from the threats and cruel machinations of the prince. By their very nature, she and the prince were at odds. His arrogance and insatiable appetites conflicted with her very being. "You will be mine," he told her as he glided toward her among the pillars of their home. She fled, to refuse him.

She knew she was still too young to face him down. She knew the confrontation was unavoidable. She knew that day would determine her fate. It wouldsurely happen, but not yet.

So, she fled.

When she was very young, so very young... she fled.

Underneath the jungle, heavily adorned with leaf, vine, and tree roots, lay the remnants of buildings. Long ago fallen into cellars. The orchards and gardens had surrendered their bounty to the encroaching wilderness like a conquered nation paying tribute— subservient and servile to the new master. What remained in this place was sufficient to fulfil her needs. Amid these treasures, she grew: wild and unfamiliar with the ways of men, but a princess none-the-less.

Regal and alert when she needed to be; joyous and playful when she wanted. It was in her blood. It was in her bones.

Each year, the prince was forced from the indolent pace of lower valley life by the monsoon rains. Torrents of rainwater cascaded down the hillsides to burst the river banks and forced him into the hills. Rarely, though, would he venture as far as her sanctuary. During those times, trembling but silent, she would hide from his continuous earnest questing. With the returning sun again heating the land and with vapour steaming off the hills, the prince returned to his easy life by the river. She returned to her easy life in the ruins.

Thus the pattern of her life seemed set. Seasons of joy followed by seasons of fear.

Oblivious to this cycle, so insignificant compared to the cycle of nations, events far away in the world of men coalesced. Disastrous events. Hearts blazed with hatred and murderous intent. War took hold of reason and shredded it beyond recognition. Any rationality that remained gave justification only to further irrational violence. Over time, like the disease it was, the war spread. Even to the quiet river settlements far removed from the conflict's origin, it came.

Beneath the downpour in yet another monsoon season, she gazed timidly from beneath dripping foliage. This much rain would surely bring the prince again. Closer than before. She felt this strongly, but this year she felt strong in herself. This year, she did not fear him. This year, they would meet. She felt this in her blood, in her bones.

As she sat in quiet affirmation, her world was shattered by sounds beyond her understanding. Accustomed to monsoon lighting and thunder, these deafening bursts of hellish destruction buffeted herears. The war among men had come to the hillside. Galvanized by primal self-preservation, by primal fear, she fled to the deepest part of her sanctuary.

The battle gripped and bedevilled the jungle all around. Terrified she cowered beneath the stones that now trembled as much as she did. In this fray, though quarter was sometimes begged by combatants of either side, it was never given. This was a battle of obliteration. The wounded were savagely slain when discovered by either side.

Few soldiers survived the clash.

One was determined to.

Oozing life from many wounds, his weapons damaged and useless, the soldier dragged himself through mud. The rain bathed his body and washed away his blood. He crawled under brush and fallen trees, inching and sliding away from the battle in the mud.

Abruptly, the ground slipped from beneath himand he rolled into a cavity. He was delivered harshly into the hidden ruins of an ancient estate—her sanctuary. Blackness overcame him.

She stared at him from her corner, wide eyes glistening, too afraid to move, trying to meld into the stone at her back.

At length, he moaned. He stirred and grunted in pain. He pushed himself into a semi-reclining position. Shifting again into less painful repose, he warily surveyed the canopy above him and listened. No battle sounds reached him. Either it was finally finished or it was beyond range. He was safe for now.

Scanning his immediate surroundings, he started with a jerk. Her liquid eyes blinked at him from her hiding spot. His involuntary yelp frightened her. She shrank back against the rough remains of a wall, trying to make herself small, and watching him warily.

The sounds he uttered then were guttural gibberish to her. She understood his intent when he threw something to land just in front of her. Gingerly, daintily, she retrieved the morsel but swiftly retreated to safety. One nibble and her taste buds exploded in delight. Its salty sweetness confounded her tongue and defied identification. The rest of the treat vanished into her mouth. Lost in momentary bliss, she was barely aware of the man's low chuckle, but she was instantly aware of the sound of a second morsel landing in a puddle a little further from her hiding spot. Darting forward, she retrieved it and found it suffered only slightly from its watery landing.

In this way, the soldier coaxed her into the open where they regarded each other with honest appraisal.

Dim memory spoke to her of this manner of man. Like some of those in the river settlements, beneath the burden of his profession this was a gentle man, versed in the practice of kindness. She could not understand the words he intoned in a low, soothing baritone. She knew with certainly, however, he meant her no harm.

It struck her that his gift of hospitality must be reciprocated. She climbed a thick vine out of their haven, stopped, and listened. Sounds from the battle no longer pierced the jungle. In their absence, the thrumming of hard rainfall and boom of natural thunder again commanded the night. Into the wet darkness, illuminated by frequent lightning, she sprang to search for savouriness in the abandoned orchard.

Returning triumphantly, as she knew she would, she approached the soldier timidly. He lay still, eyes half-closed, breathing painfully, lost in his private world of thought, suffering, and fatigue. She placed her offering within his reach and dashed backward, watching him. Her swift movement returned him to alertness. Peering down at her offering, he uttered a grunting sound that turned into a wet cough. Exhausted, he lay his head back and fell asleep.

Glancing repeatedly between him and her offering, it became obvious to her that he would not be availing himself of the delicious supper she found. So, she ate it herself, biting into and consuming the juicy sweet flesh with relish.

Morning's arrival brought only slightly less darkness under continued deluge. Although it did provide some shelter from the downpour, their refuge was not untouched by it. Water cascaded down vegetation-covered stones that had long ago slipped from their original placement. It fell like a curtain into the center of their sanctuary. Their haven did not fill with the life-choking flood. Rather, it drained away to join the torrents rushing to swell the river below.

Her thoughts turned to the prince. Would he flee that watery advance soon? Was he already on his way? From what direction would he approach?

The soldier stirred in his sleep. She turned her gaze upon him. He suffered. That was apparent even in his slumber. She did not know what to do. She knew no arts to heal him. He must be healed or he must die. She didn't want him to die. That would foul her sanctuary and she would have to leave.

He stirred again and inhaled in sharp pain. The sound stirred something deep within her. Easing forward, she dared touch his hand. When that brought no response, she touched his face. A gentle touch, a touch of concern.

His eyes opened. He gazed at her in surprise, then tenderness. Sounds again flowed from his lips. She still could not understand. Tilting her head, she regarded him. When he shifted his body, she jumped away. He reached into his treasure trove and brought forward another piece of that treat from last night. Breaking it in two, he offered her half. Daring beyond sense, she reached forward and took it in gratitude. They dined. Breakfast for two under the monsoon rain.

Food strengthen him enough so that he could assess his own wounds. The pain of moving, however, left him panting and angry. He slammed his fists into the ground in frustration and shouted at the air.

His shouts sent her fleeing upward out of their haven, going anywhere but there. Into the jungle, she fled this suddenly changed being. The jungle was filled with creatures she knew. The man was a creature she did not know. Slowing her pace, however, she found she could not stop thinking about him. He was hurt. He was kind in spite of his pain. He was helpless. The prince was coming.

She stopped.

The prince was coming.

She retraced her path in a panic. The prince was coming. The prince would kill the man. This she knew for certain. Driven away from his comfortable home by the floods, the prince would be in a foul mood. The prince in a foul mood would strike at anything he found. The prince would kill the man.

She could not bear this to happen. The man was her treasure. She should not have left him helpless.

Racing back to the ruins, her heart nearly burst with terror when she heard them. The prince uttered his proclamation of doom to the man, answered by the man's shout of fear and defiance. Leaping down over the edge of ruin, she knocked the prince away from his intended victim. She rolled away and rose to face the prince. To that dreaded prince, the demon prince with his crown encircling his head held so high, she declared her resolve, "No! You will not kill him!"

Hissing his disdain, the prince struck at her with his poisoned weapons. Dancing aside, she launched her counterattack, sliced into his body with hardened and honed nails, and danced away again. The man shouted and tried to help by throwing stones and mud at the prince. Ignoring him, the two combatants twisted around and struck each other, time and time again, until blood flowed freely and the prince, with a final release of breath, shuddered and lay still.

She was not untouched, however. The prince's poison burned in her veins. The day had come. Her fate was determined. With her own sigh, she lay down to die. In that moment, she felt her body being lifted by the man. To her adoring amazement, he cradled herclose and wept.

* * *

He had come with this war to this land with its strange mythologies, compelled by promises of righteous deeds, envied reputation, and riches. Whathe became immersed in was vicious slaughter and fear.The only riches he gleaned were a few near-worthless baubles from the corpses of those he had slain. He was trapped by vows and by law. He was deep into it now and the only value he could hope for from the whole bloody mess was to get out alive, maybe with a few more baubles in his pockets.

He fought on, as did those other fools who had been duped into this venture. One by one, or in screaming mangled groups, those he knew were slain in this farce. Their faces were replaced by strangers and he fought, a stranger even to himself, among a company of strangers.

Yesterday's battle was merely another in a theme, soon to be relegated to the closet of haunting memories. And, may the gods of this land be kind, never remembered. Gods of any land were rarely kind.

This morning had come with more of that damnable rain. At least the ruins were situated on the hillside so the rain drained away. He'd been lucky so far. He wasn't dead yet. He had shelter of sorts and some food in his knapsack. And he had friendly company. That was the biggest surprise.

He didn't mean to frighten her away. He was badly hurt, though, and not going anywhere soon. He was going to die in this fetid jungle pit if somebody, the right somebody, didn't find him. That meant shouting for help.

His shouting scared away his new companion. What he didn't count on, was what it brought.

He looked up and saw the cobra, hissing and hood flared, eager to attack. Fear and panic stabbed his heart. As the cobra reared back to strike him, his companion leapt down and knocked it aside.

The battle was on. Each twisted and spun around the other, neither one asking nor giving any quarter. Their savagery was a match to the battle of the day before. But here, he was the object being fought over. She fought for him. Her valour made yesterday's slaughter a mockery.

He cursed his useless weapon left back in the jungle somewhere. He cursed his legs that wouldn't move. He flung rocks and mud to drive the damnable enemy away. He raged at the unfairness.

Oblivious to the rain pounding into this battleground, the combatants fought on. Water splashed and whirled around them, playing tricks with light and blurring their forms. Half-delirious from pain-fevered brow and fear, he saw the combatants change. She took ennobled form. His champion became a princess… —no, the shining spirit of a goddess. The cobra became a demon prince, the epitome of the evil that had taken root within his own self. In the eyes of the cobra, he saw every foe he fought. More horrifically, he saw his own eyes glaring back at him, filled with hatred and murder. She fought not just for his life. The light of her love fought to vanquish the darkness in the war-tainted soldier's soul.

Then it was done. The cobra lay dead and she lay dying.

With sudden awesome and fearful awareness, his heart broke at the depth of her sacrifice.

Gathering the wee mongoose into his hands, he cradled her and wept. To his surprise, she opened her eyes and he saw the love in their depths before life faded from her.

That was how his compatriots found him, drawn by his shouts while they searched for survivors from yesterday's battle. They carried him away to tend his wounds. He lived and served for many years, rising in rank and accomplishment. Over the years, the band of men became a regiment. To this day, the regimental crest bears the depiction of a mongoose slaying a cobra, for he had never tired of telling the story of the mongoose's bravery and sacrifice.

***

That is the story, the history, behind this moment. And so I speak to you now. Heart to heart.

Know this: the powers that change you take on many forms. We are not always aware of their true nature. But sometimes, the most powerful, those that will not be denied, are laid plainly and painfully before our vision. Welcome the change, the gift, and transcend what you were.

Be kind. Be gentle. Be loving and caring. Be of strong body and stout heart. Be clear of mind and purpose. Train hard. Train well. And, should you ever carry this escutcheon into battle, remember this: you fight not for yourself, but for those behind you. Those who cannot fight.

The words on the crest: Vide Cor Meum? They mean: Behold My Heart. Do everything with Love and you will win every time, even if you die.

Welcome to the Order of the Mongoose.

Thomas Keesman

Thomas Keesman has been a constant reader since early childhood. At twelve, he decided to write science fiction. Now retired from provincial public service, he finally gets to do just that.

Keesman draws on life, historical events, and an overactive sense of 'well, what if?' for his stories. He often explores how marginalized individuals cope with the challenges of both daily life and extraordinary change. Throughout, there is a sense the characters and writer have agreed to respect each other's lives beyond the story.

His first novel *Extraordinaire* was published in 2013. His current project is a collection of linked short stories. Keesman lives in Victoria BC.

The Farmer Takes a Wife

Whatever is true of a thing is true of its like.

Studies in Deductive Logic: W. S. Jevons

"Four data runs, the same two first-place candidates: Ballantine twice, Simpson twice. After all this time, picking your wife comes down to apreference in T's and A's."

Georges deMarck cleared his throat as he dropped the summary from the handwriting expert on the table. The graphoanalysist made extensive comments on each candidate, noting Phyllis Ballantine's capital T's revealed a sharp mind in economic and political analysis, circumscribed by good-humoured discipline. Delores Simpson's A's, he went on, demonstrated no less intelligence, which would best complement her formidable design skills.

Technically, the little native was correct. But tone, word choice and expression made his casual comment sound obscene. "You are quite disgusting, Waugh."

"True, true. My sense of humor makes you uncomfortable. But at least I have one. I would point out that I am not the one who..." The lab assistant stopped, sighed, rolled his shoulders to loosen them, then peered up at deMarck.

"I am not involved in this because of your skulking little political officer. You know I admire Lord Jevons, for both his teaching and technical abilities. He was a true extraordinaire, right up to that final descent into insanity. But he was inspired and inspiring. And I have the honor to know one of his daughters - your dark master's wife.

She invited me to tea, made a case for the potential usefulness of this project, then asked me to participate. Given who she is, had she asked me to walk through fire, I would have done so gladly." One unruly eyebrow wiggled. "Well, maybe not that."

"Georges, you have put me through hell with this project. Regardless of his position, Schott can invoke that "Officers of the Law Courts" provision only so long. Frankly, I weary of the threats of a hard labor residency on the Isle of Man. The professor's friends in London would make hay in Westminster with questions regarding the Empire's machinery andmanpower being used for matchmaking.

"The professor can blow smoke. Ha! The professor *is* smoke." Their well-worn dispute was interrupted by three jarring notes from the door buzzer. Waugh frowned as he glanced at the clock above the blackboard. It was far too early for deliveries, no appointments were scheduled that day and uninvited visitors were forbidden. Yet it was the correct two-buzzes-pause-then-one sequence.

With a sharp look at his visitor, Waugh moved to a framed bird's-eye perspective map of Victoria, grasped the side of the hinged frame and swung it out of the way. The shallow recess behind the print housed an adjustable four-inch lens, a wheel and a two-position slide.

Waugh spun the wheel, flooding light through the camera obscura. A projected image of the hallway appeared on the opposite wall. Waugh moved the slide back and forth. The first position provided a front view of the caller. The second provided a side view. They saw a boy about 12 standing patiently, holding an envelope in both hands.

Waugh whispered, "Ronsey. One of my errand boys." Reading the depth of his disquiet, deMarck drew his pistol - not normally an appropriate response in civil conversations, but seldom the wrong one in thecircles he traveled. He stood back from the bank of windows, looking for threats.

No one was near the building. An automobile was parked two houses down; where a woman sat in the open car speaking to two young girls on the sidewalk. When his scan was complete, Georges turned his attention back to the electric vehicle, which sported the distinctive headlamp array of the California Automobile Works. Money there. He turned back to Waugh, shaking his head. Little more than 15 seconds had passed from door buzzer to head shake.

"Hello. Who is there, please?" When he saw deMarck begin to pocket the gun, Waugh flicked a hand impatiently. Georges brought the gun to bear onthe door.

"Mr. Hugh. It's Peter Ronsey, sir. Got paid to bring an envelope by."

"Ronsey, Herr Professor is away for another two weeks. I cannot accept anything on his behalf. You know that."

"It's not for the Professor, Mr. Hugh. The lady who gave it over - with an American half dollar - she said to put it into the hands of Mister Saint Hubert Waugh hisself. Is your name really Saint Hubert?"

"Never mind, Ronsey. However, I am certain no literate adult would say 'hisself'. Let me open up." Waugh spun the wheel in the opposite direction to close the iris, snapped the print back in place, then glanced around to ensure nothing telling was in sight. He made a noisy production of unlocking the door.

The boy, who had run the occasional message for Waugh, waited without complaint. The neighborhood kids pretty much agreed the little Indian, queer in the head with rules about everything, had his good points - first among them being good pay for easy errands. Once in, the boy immediately handed over the envelope, then stood back.

The irregularity of the situation made Waugh uncomfortable. He held the envelope by diagonal corners, hefting it, running a finger along the sealed flap, then holding it near an electric light for any clues. All the while, the fluid motion of brows, eyes and pursed lips signaled his puzzlement. Georges felt vaguely seasick from watching those brows. Finally,

Waugh tore an end off to shake the contents out. So focused on the mystery in hand, he only then asked about its origin.

"Me and Askey and a couple of others were over by the cricket pitch, when this C.A.W. electric came coasting up. It stopped near us and this swank lady, American accent but not a Puget one, asked if we knew where Professor Knecht's offices might be. When we pointed across the park, she asked if one of us would deliver a message for 50 cents. We did paper-rock-scissors. I won."

At the mention of the California Automobile Works, deMarck's head snapped up. "You, over here." Despite his size and the authoritative tone, the boy didn't move. As Georges began to repeat the order, the boy interrupted.

"This is Mr. Hugh's lab, and his rules. I don't do nothing here without his say. Or the Professor's, if he ever shows up." He looked back at Waugh, whose mouth quivered just shy of a smile. Waugh lifted the fuzzy caterpillar over one eye, and the boy walked over to stand near the window, but out of reach.

Georges pointed. "That her?" The boy looked surprised, nodded. Georges was not. He had employed this technique often enough himself: prowl the area where the target has gone to ground, ask boys on the street if they knew where so and so lived, commission the delivery of a note, tail them to the site. He wouldn't be surprised if the envelope was empty - his had often been. This one was not.

Waugh held a single sheet of Mount Baker Hotel letterhead. The earlier dance of eyebrows and lips was repeated, joined now by a hum at the end of each sentence he read. When he finished, he dismissed the boy, grudgingly matching the extravagant half dollar payout. When they were alone, he spoke in a subdued tone.

"When I was first dragooned into this undertaking, I was furious with you. At our first meeting you declared superior intelligence as the first qualifier, and I had hope for you. Now," he waved the page at deMarck "I think I pity you."

"This is from your Miss Phyllis Ballantine of Dubuque. It informs me that the Misses Ballantine and Simpson independently breached the project safeguards - one directly, the other through an agent. That would be the break in at our hidden Seattle office at the midpoint of the second iteration. Miss Simpson removed the criteria folders and made copies. As she returned the papers the next night, she came face to face with Simpson's agent. A lively correspondence culminated in Miss Ballantine relocating to San Francisco as a houseguest of Delores Simpson. They are now the best of friends."

Georges looked stricken. This is not how it should have played out at all. There were protocols, blind mail drops and decoy locations built in to prevent both the revelation of the project and possible contact between candidates. He could almost see the headlines in the gutter press. Dear God, if they mentioned Mr. Schott, Georges would be lucky to be begging on the streets. Waugh cleared his throat.

"There is more. She has lodging in Oak Bay for the next three days. She requests you take lunch with her. Today. This provides a description of herself and her automobile, both of which appear to be what we see parked outside." Waugh nearly giggled, in hysteria far more than humor. "The tables are turned, Georges. It seems you are the interviewee."

Horrified as he was, Georges was not hesitant by nature. He straightened tie and jacket on his way to the door. He barely heard Waugh's "good luck" as he strode across the lawn. Phyllis Ballantine looked up, smiled, and said something to the children who moved off, the younger one waving shyly. Turning to him, she extended her hand.

"Georges, how very nice to meet you in person." A handshake that managed to be neither mannish nor feminine. Interesting. "Our agent reports you have a strong interest and aptitude in the mechanical arts, including automobiles. Can you manage a wheel instead of a steering bar? I will explain what we are doing today. There are three areas we are interestedin: what you assembled, how and why."

She saw he was ready to drive and suggested they make their way toward Oak Bay. "Since I am sure there will be a great deal of detail, we may as well take that scenic drive I've read about. Now, to business. You've put together an impressive arsenal of technology, then applied it in an innovative way.

"The logic work is decidedly that of Professor Hermes Knecht, so says Dolly. The intelligence gathering framework is quite robust, doubtlessly related to your Colonial Office function.

"Other than adding graphology in the last iteration, we could only guess at the rest of it. Some pretty informed guessing but please, tell me what you've done."

He outlined how he arrived at his criteria. When he began to talk about why, she gently suggested they get the technical aspects out of the way. He went on to his discussions with his employer about how to gather and manage the necessary data. Phyllis swallowed a snort when he mentioned how Thomas Schott had requested his own wife join them in the planning. She shook her head at his questioning glance, signaling him to continue.

Once they had the criteria, Georges was introduced to Saint Hubert Waugh to craft solid questions and a sound evaluation framework. They used a Jevons logic piano to test the responses to each series of questions. Finally, the data was stored on punched Korsakov cards, for later sorting with the Russian's reader.

Even as they waded through the mountain of paper generated by the third series, they realized further information was required. Georges was drawn by the possibilities of graphology. But Waugh had been quite firm about the under-developed nature of the discipline, and prevailed in using it as an adjunct - a 'tie-breaker' as it were.

Georges had warmed to the topic. The nods and sounds Phyllis offered encouraged him to talk about the project's worthiness in its own right. That view must have been most evident in the way he spoke of Hugh Waugh. She asked just how he convinced Professor Knecht, renowned for his crankiness, to lend both equipment and assistant.

Georges enjoyed her surprise on learning Hermes Knecht was a creation of Hugh Waugh, who posed as his hapless assistant. The bright little tribal boy from up-coast caught the attention of the CoE missionaries, who recognized his potential. They sent him first to Toronto, then on to University College in London, where he was awarded degrees in numerics and logic. On returning home, he found his co-tribalists wary of a man too immersed in alien concepts, the missionaries disappointed in his lack of theological leaning, and an academic community chilly toward a smart Native. After a few months he left Vancouver, invented Knecht and set up shop on the edges of civilization, as Victoria was widely regarded.

"Oh my lord, the Knecht Modification is his?" Seeing his blank look, she went on. "It reduced the number of keys needed for the logic piano. Knecht - I mean Waugh - hinged the vertical rods so the keys could be pushed in or left in their default position. With a second position, each key can register either the truth or falsity of a statement. Thus a four statement submission is represented by four keys rather than the eight Lord Jevons originally built in. It means little even at the eight key level, but modern machines deal with upwards of several hundred statements. With the original configuration, operators faced a wall of keys. The potential for errors multiplies exponentially as the number of keys increase. Brilliant, oh so brilliant. Dolly would be thrilled to meet him."

"Dolly? You've mentioned that name twice now."

"My pet name for Delores. She corresponded with Knecht occasionally, and was disappointed to learn he was out of town for the month. I take it he is usually unreachable?" She laughed at deMarck's expression.

"Er. Yes. Dolly knows you are here? With me?"

Again the soft laugh. "Of course. We have a business venture of our own. Dolly is investigating an opportunity in Portland, while I interview you. Working separately allows us to cover twice the territory. Of course that only works where there is absolute trust between the partners. Also, our experience has been that initial discussions are more focused with a two-person conversation."

"As in fewer keys, fewer errors. How am I doing so far?"

"I don't believe you would ask a teacher that in the middle of an examination." The smile again. "However, this is not freshman year, and you are not sitting Latin grammar. You have demonstrated outstanding skills. Your method points to a worthwhile mindset. Your response to this unexpected turn of events has been flexible, without fear. So far, you are confirming your place as most qualified among our correspondents."

"And being a good correspondent is a desirable thing?"

"Quite, although the word stands proxy for a number of qualities. In the literal sense, Dolly is a legendary letter writer. And a common correspondent helped bring us together in mutual interest. The late Vera Bogdanovskaia was a polymath with whom I exchanged thoughts on the structure of unarticulated language elements, which in turn informed my understanding of the vocabulary of international finance. Dolly was in the early stages of coauthoring an entomology text with her until Vera unfortunately blew herself up a couple of years ago. Gone far too early.

"But let us return to you. I will do my best to answer every question you might have, but we'll do that over lunch. You must have amassed considerable data, given the exhaustive series of questionnaires." She changed gears. In a tone he could only describe as deeply serious, she asked why he set up his own search the way he did. "Here's your opportunity to speak to motives. Tell all you can. Take your time."

Georges had followed the shoreline scenic route. On Sundays and holidays, it would take on the appearance of a conveyor belt - an endless procession of carriages moving auto-promenaders en masse from

Beacon Hill to the gates of Governor's Park on McNeill Bay. Mid-week, they had the route to themselves. They neared the crest of Gonzales Hill, with its fine panorama of city, sea and the Olympics beyond. He steered the electric to a level parking area, overlooking the strait. In silence he handed her out then led the way to the lookout shelter.

While sorting his thoughts, a corner of his mind rebelled at being interrogated. That faded almost instantly. In fairness, she had every right to ask what he would have in her place. And this was hardly a cellar interrogation. Under the fading resentment was a certain rawness in talking about his failed marriage

He stood beside her, thrust his hands deep into his pants pockets, and stared off in the direction of the American mountains. Georges spoke in a near conversational manner, recounting the lightening courtship and how they married with love-stars in their eyes. And how his love was utterly crushed when she walked out on him less than a year later. He believed the majority of people were happier with a mate - and that he would be. But this time, he vowed, he would not be blinded by his heart. Logic would govern his selection process.

"And?"

Over the course of the last year and a half, as he moved ever closer to a logical choice, he also found the assembly and coordination were satisfying activities in themselves. He looked a bit embarrassed at that admission. Then he chuckled.

"My employer's wife, Lou, is his, ah, associate in the office. When we began, she looked over what Waugh and I laid out. I only just found out that she convinced Hugh Waugh to participate in my project. Lou asked questions, and made some very good suggestions. Then she shared what her grandpa Jack liked to say: the two biggest kinds of fool are those who think with their hearts, and those who feel with their brains. So long as I kept that in mind, she felt I would do fine."

Georges was surprised when Phyllis gently took his hand. He hadn't realized she had moved to his side. Or that he had taken his hands out of his pockets. Self-conscious of how much he gestured when talking, Georges usually kept his hands jammed into jacket or pants pockets.

"Oh Georges, this looks more and more promising. I have a 'Louise story' to relate as well. But I will share that over lunch." She held on to his hand as she continued.

"Dolly has quite a good sense about innovation in business, with generous access to the Mortonfortunes. That would be the North CaliforniaMortons, as they don't talk to the Los Angeles clan at all. Dolly married a Simpson of the SoCal Battery family. He died in the explosion that leveled their Mexico City plant. She returned to San Francisco and the family business. She soon took over the design office for new models. Success upon success allowed the Morton family to swallow up their major competitors, then rebrand their expanded enterprise as California Automobile Works.

"The Morton brothers are surprisingly eager to invest in Dolly's outside business ventures. I suspect they would be more comfortable with her disengaged from C.A.W. and out of their hair. Better yet, out of the country. Their loss."

"The three of us have a range of compatible skills. I am here to see how far that compatibility extends."

"There is a wondrous variety among geniuses. One can be a brilliant theorist, such as your Mr. Waugh. One can be a mechanical marvel, able to build anything, the Edisons of the world. Then we have those who do not possess any technical skills - or not more than a modicum - but who can gather a number of technologies, then make them work together. You might modestly argue that it was Waugh who did this. But my investigator says he is not innovative by nature. Well that is not quite accurate if, as you say, he fabricated Knecht in order to work unmolested. Not unlike Dolly and me, in some ways. I digress."

"So you have played me? Did you coordinate your responses to test me?"

"Not at all, Georges. We completed the forms without consultation, and continued to do so after we met. Later, in reflecting on our answers, we gained valuable insight into ourselves and each other. Those insights helped spark a possible joint business venture. We might never have met but for your project. For that, if nothing else, we owe you thanks. Well, that and those files store at your Seattle operation. We've made a few casual contacts with other talented candidates - without spilling the beans on your work, of course. I think we may forge a few business alliances out of that information."

"Dolly and I quickly found the major frustration in our lives to be the strictures of proper society. They stifle us intellectually, socially and economically. Aside from Woodhull and her sister, an example waved under my nose more than I care for, economic and political prospects for American women are practically nil. Things are only slightly better in either England or Canada. Australia slavishly follows the masculine script. We would not consider settling in many other places. The top of our list - which we arrived atseparately - is New Zealand.

"I am not even convinced it is all that progressive in spirit, but it is small and distant. We know the Empire engineered its dominion status, and it serves asa safely isolated social laboratory. First, they treated with the Maori instead of exterminating them as they did the Hottentots. Ten years later, they tried out emancipation for Catholiques, then Hebrews. Finally, six years ago, they granted suffrage to women. At every turn, they tried something out, watched what happened, then moved on if it didn't blow up.

"We need a place that will give us breathing room, allow us participation as full citizens. What is it that dreary old Canadian judge said - women are not persons in the law. So, we are seeking a partner; one who can take leaps, one with an open mind, one with a sense for the application of practical technology in business."

"And you believe New Zealand will give you room to grow. How will you work in the longer term, given the strictures you named?"

"We are on the verge of the twentieth century. I am confident that all these outdated notions will be vanquished and forgotten by the onset of the twenty-first. Good riddance is all I can say to that. As to how you fit in, and I know you did not ask out loud, we will speak to that after lunch.

"Hmm, busy lunch," he murmured.

"Indeed. But mull this. Your current position would be undermined by an alliance with either the Simpsons or the Ballantines. You may need to leap again. Dolly found that most intriguing - your ability to leap when the time is right. The story we've compiled says you left England when the situation became too hot. You abandoned the skirt-chasing souse who came to Canada with you. You leaped into the unknown when you joined Mr. Thomas Schott, without any experience in personal security. You've jumped repeatedly. And thrived.

"On bouncing back from a disastrous marriage you undertook a daring project - which called from some pretty spirited defense among hostile decision-makers. These are all good things, Georges. We needed to meet you face to face, and to get a sense of the man behind those bold moves."

"We are nearly there. I've reserved a private dining room." She frowned slightly. "Dolly did ask me to follow up on one detail that eluded our agents. One of your American counterparts referred to you as Farmer George. Is there more to that than you being a farmer when you met Mr. Schott?"

He laughed. "That would be Henry Page of Pinkerton. To be accurate, I was not a farmer. I was working on a farm. Between leaps, so to speak."

They left the electric with an attendant, enjoyed an unhurried lunch, punctuated by wide-ranging conversation. Later, on the veranda overlooking the strait, Phyllis Ballantine laid out a stack of sheets. Dolly had prepared a series of questions to which Georges was asked to respond with the first thing that came to mind. At first, Phyllis took extensive notes. That dwindled to an occasional underlining of keywords. Finally, she simply listened.

Later, she brought up the complete range of choices before him. In her orderly way, she presented a logical progression: neither A nor B; A not B; B not A; both A and B. Still later, after the logical progression had been thoroughly discussed, she suggested a light meal before continuing. There were still capacities and compatibilities to be assessed.

***

Georges woke before five and washed and dressed as quietly as he could. He mused that 24 hours before he could not have imagined possibilities that now seemed the most sensible of all. As he pulled on his shoes, Phyllis emerged from the bedroom, clad in a silk wrapper but still barefoot. She walked him to the top of the service stairs.

"That was as enjoyable as a necessity could have been." To his raised brow, she continued, "Make no mistake, Georges, this is not an invitation to some free love colony run by penniless anarchists. Nor are you setting up as some Old Testament patriarch. Here is a gateway to a whole life approach to economic, intellectual and personal satisfaction – not an answer for everyone, but right for us. We don't know what it looks like on the other side of that gateway. We need to trust and work with - in all ways - whoever crosses that divide in our company."

Phyllis had booked passage to Honolulu on a steamer, saying it would allow for a final determination of their compatibility. The Hawaiian layover would allow Georges to make his return if he found the prospects unacceptable. He firmly declined the out. "In for a penny, as they say." She smiled, saying it was also a checkpoint for her and Dolly: Look before you leap, as they also say. Georges grinned, kissed her cheek and departed with a silence unusual for a man his size.

He was briefly tempted to stroll along in the cool of the morning. Instead, he set off at a quick pace, making directly for Professor Knecht's laboratory. He arrived well before Waugh's normal arrival. He let himself in, then sat in the sun near the window. An hour later, the doorknob turned. Waugh opened the door before realizing it was unlocked. "Hello? Is someone there, please?"

"Well, it's not Peter Ronsey, Waugh."

Waugh threw the door open and stood wide-eyed.

"Waugh, why are you wearing a basket on your head?"

"Please Georges, it is a traditional hat of my people, which I take some small comfort in. On a practical level, it enables me to move about nearly invisibly - unless I walk too near children or look like I'm about to beg for money. Wait. How did you get in?"

"For all your mirrors and other trickery that lock was disappointingly easy to pick. Say, shouldn't that thing be some sort of turbine?" At the scowl on the brown face George added, "In any event, I am here to discuss a sizeable hole in your logic, as well as the end of our work."

Waugh hung the woven hat in a cupboard as he spoke. "You are very insulting for someone who came to this with poorly shaped ideas and a ridiculous desire to misapply logic to love. First, wrong Indians. Second, the headwear you so blithely insult is a turban. A turbine is a propeller turned by water to generate electricity. I beg your pardon. What do you mean the end of our work?"

"You are very good at your work, Waugh. But sometimes important connections are overlooked by the best of us. For instance, Miss Simpson openly provided the information that she was a widow. We correctly assumed she retained her late husband's name, but gave little consideration to her maiden name. She was born Delores Marie Morton, as in Morton Motors. Which later became California Automobile Works. Where, until lately, she headed the design office. You will no doubt recall corresponding with Del Morton on an air resistance calculation. Said Del Morton wishes to meet you face to face when she arrives in the next couple of days."

Waugh had removed his coat, but only gripped it as he tried to follow the barrage of information.

"As it happens, you were not her sole Vancouver Island correspondent. She and Louise Schott have exchanged letters for nearly ten years. Phyllis also has a previous connection with Lou. The way she mentioned it, I felt it was wise to leave that in the shadows. She did say that Louise had a pretty broad view of other household arrangements. I must have looked a bit stunned, so she told me outright about Louise's previous household was made up of her and her two, hmm, partners - Bert and Davey. That was in its final throes when Thomas came on the scene. Lou gave Phyllis explicit permission to share this with me, if it contributed to an intelligent decision. Said you were fully in the know, but that you were the soul of discretion.

"So it seems I owe Lou as much as you do her father, just not in the same way. "

Georges moved to the black board. He stood facing it, hefting a piece of yellow chalk. He looked over his shoulder in mock severity. "Now as to your failings in logic. Recall how you lectured me - with endless diagrams - that all two-element statements encompass four expressions. It is an odd thing to be the layman correcting the expert. But rather pleasingat the same time."

He turned to the board, and scrawled:

1) Neither A nor B

2) A, not B

3) B, not A

4) Both A and B

He drew a heavy double line under the last one, then dropped the chalk on the ledge beside a dusty eraser. He smiled as he looked around the room. "Best start wrapping up, Waugh. The project is a success. I will leave my current position within hours, bound for Auckland the day after tomorrow."

It all dawned on Saint Hubert Waugh in that instant. Dropping the coat he was about to hang, he nearly shouted. "Both? You're marrying both of them? You?"

***

Georges resigned his position that afternoon, gratified by Mr. Schott's prepared letter of recommendation. He met quietly with his employer's wife to offer a personal thanks. Phyllis telegraphed the agency with instructions to terminate the Simpson-Ballantine research project. She also confirmed Dolly's flights for the next day: Portland to Seattle, Seattle to Victoria. That allowed a day and a half to see the local sights, as well as complete the wind up of their North American affairs.

Their passage to Honolulu was by way of a comfortably large steamer. Phyllis reasoned that ten days of thorough discussion would establish a solid ground rules for the new partnership.

Hardly a story of love at first sight, you say? There are many paths a thoughtful and likeminded group might follow to create a once in a lifetime opportunity. This one involved a simple but complete range of solutions and time to consider the data. After that, as with all human enterprises, what they do with their solution is entirely up to them.

Vince Galati

Victoria based writer Vince Galati lives with his girlfriend Donna, his number one audience and his muse. A Dream Infernal was conceived and born during a meeting of the Eclectic Writer's Boot Camp. It is the second short story published for the transplanted Ontarian and he continues to work toward publishing a novel.

A Dream Infernal

Andy woke with a painful stiffness in his loins. He gripped his erection in an attempt to ease the pressure. He'd dreamed about her again, the woman who'd haunted his sleep for more than a month. She oozed sex, every little bit of her from the way she walked to the little upturn of her lips when she smiled. He didn't normally remember his dreams so vividly. Each one seemed more real than the last. Yesterday, he could still smell her when he woke, could taste her cherry lip gloss. He let go of himself and found a single long hair entwined in his fingers. He often found long blond hairs in his crotch, but this one was red.

He sat up with a start and shook his hand, trying to dislodge the hair so Gemma wouldn't find it. It was bad enough that he'd called her Freya last night. He watched the hair fall, marveling at how it caught the morning light peeking through the small space between the curtains and seemed to hold it as it twisted and weaved its way to the floor. He swung his legs over the edge of the bed and dropped his feet to the floor, one on either side of the hair. He bent down and picked it back up. Holding it between his fingers, he brought it to his nose and sniffed it. It was impossible, but it smelled like her. He inhaled deeply. He couldn't help himself.

"What are you doing?" Gemma said. She was sitting up against the wall, rubbing the sleep out her eyes. Andy rolled the strand of hair into his fist as quick as he could, and found his composure. He stood up and turned to face his girlfriend, greeting her with his still rock hard member.

Gemma grinned, seemingly having forgotten about last night's debacle. "Oh, somebody's awake," she began. "Too bad Freya isn't here." Then again, maybe not. Andy was stricken by her statement and his heart started to race. He teetered but caught himself, managing to make it look like he was shifting his weight from one foot to the other. He calmed, realizing she didn't really know what was going on. He frowned.

"I've gotta piss." He got up and headed for the bathroom. He put the strand of hair in the toilet and flushed, then he relieved himself, unwilling to go onthe hair.

The rest of the morning went by without a single word spoken. Andy had a shower and dressed while Gemma made herself breakfast. Then they switched. Andy was out of the house and on his way to work before Gemma was finished with her morning rituals. This was the way it usually went, but before today, at least there was some conversation and a kiss when they crossed paths. Last night's episode had caused irrevocable damage to their relationship. Andy had felt it slipping away for a while. He didn't look at Gemma the same anymore. He couldn't, not since he started dreaming of the fiery-haired woman. He hadn't stopped sleeping with Gemma. If anything they had more sex in the past month. When Andy dreamed of Freya, he was filled with insatiable lust which often wouldn't subside with just one go. He couldn't finish it himself either. The pressure would build until he had intercourse.

Andy sat on the bus on the way to the subway station. He couldn't get the last dream out of his head. It was never easy to evict thoughts of Freya from his mind. The feeling in his loins was unbearable. It was worse than usual. Last night's dream was so vivid he could remember the feel of her silky-smooth skin. He could feel her lips on his neck, could recall her finger tips moving over his sides and hips. Most troubling was the hair. He tried to rationalize it. It must have been Gemma's, the morning light playing tricks. What about the smell? A residual memory of the dream he'd awoken from, he told himself.

He was the last person off the bus and trailed behind the crowd as they filed through the doors into the station. Andy was lost in thought, falling even further behind when he caught her scent in the air. It was too strong to be just a lingering scent. It smelled as if she was right there. It had to be her. No one else smelled like that. Surely, he was going insane. When he reached for the door, he felt her lips on his ear lobe and a soft whisper of his name. He spun around, his heart pounding. He was alone. He hurried through the doors and took the stairs two at a time down to the subway platform. He tried to forget what just happened, force it out of mind. The growing pressure in his pants didn't make it easy.

The day went by even more slowly than it normally did. Andy was stuck in his cubicle, his work finished for the day but it was still only half past eleven. He swivelled his chair back and forth and stared at his computer screen. The image on it shifting constantly as the screen saver went about its programmed course. Andy didn't see it, though. His mind was elsewhere, going over the events of the morning. He spent the better part of the rest of his shift convincing himself he was going crazy. The alternative was just a little more than he could handle.

Andy was snapped back to reality by a voice that seemed to be calling his name, muted at first as thoughhe were underwater, then he heard it clearly. Mark was standing in the entry way to the cubicle, leaning his right arm on the top of the short wall.

"Holy shit, man! Good fuckin dream or what?"

Andy rubbed his forehead and slid his hand down his face as if trying to wipe the sleepiness away. He gave his head a quick shake to clear it.

"Sorry dude. What's up?" Andy asked.

"We're gonna grab some grub at the pub and get shit-faced. You in?"

"No, I should probably—", he started before his cell phone vibrated on his desk top. He glanced at the screen. It was a message from Gemma. It read: Lunch at Nick's. We need to talk. "On second thought, I have a feeling I'll be available."

"Trouble at home?" Mark started to ask. "You know what? Forget it. We'll get fucked and forget about whatever it is. Meet us there." Mark spun out of the cubicle and strode down the aisle back to his own work station.

Andy peeked at the message on his phone again. *Forget? I wish it were that easy.* He loved Gemma, had been with her for three years. He'd never met a woman who affected him the way she did. He should be heartbroken having his relationship falling apart at the seams as it was, but he wasn't. He still had Freya. He knew it was a ridiculous thought, but he was overwhelmed with it. Thinking of her made the feeling in his loins, the pressure, become more intense. It was painful, the need he felt. It was insane. Mark couldn't have come at a better time. He needed a drink in the worst way. Getting drunk was the only way he could think of to dull his senses enough to forget both women.

Andy sat in a booth at Nick's Italian Bistro, rolling the same meatball around in plate with his fork. He stared into his spaghetti, attempting to digest the words he'd just heard while trying to keep his food down. He felt sick, light-headed and clammy. He could barely hold his fork for how sweaty his hands had become.

Gemma sat across from him, staring at him, waiting for his response. The tension between them was palpable, made all the worse by the silence that followed Gemma telling Andy she was leaving him.

"Are you going to say anything?" Gemma asked.

"What to want me to say?" Andy answered into the best spaghetti and meatballs in town.

"Anything!" she said, throwing her hands into the air and slamming into the back rest of the booth.

It was a bit too loud. Nick's was a popular spot at lunch and today was no different. No less than twenty sets of eyes were on them now. Gemma leaned forward again and spoke more quietly.

"How about a fuck you, even? Do you even care at all? How long have you been fucking this Freya or whatever her name is?"

"I haven't been fucking anyone." His response was flat, matter of fact.

"How do you expect me to believe that?"

"I don't. I figure at this point you're going to believe whatever you want no matter what I say." Andy lifted his gaze from his lunch for the first time. "You've already decided what you're going to do. What's the point?"

"What's the point?" she asked a little louder than she intended, drawing even more eyes. "That's exactly what this is about, Andy. You don't give a shit anymore. You haven't for weeks. You've disconnected."

Andy couldn't argue that point. While it had been true that their sex life hadn't taken a hit, they weren't really talking much. They went about their daily routines, spoke when necessary and rarely engaged in any in depth conversation.

"I don't know what you want from me, Gemma, I really don't. I'm not sleeping with anyone else. You know where I am twenty-four hours a day, so I'm not sure when I'd be able to manage it anyway." He held up his hand when Gemma appeared ready to interject. "I know what you're going to say: who's Freya?" He shrugged and shook his head. "I have no idea where the name came from. So, believe me or not, you're going to draw your own conclusions and make up your own mind, which, in fact, you already have. I saw your car when I came in. You've packed more than just an overnight bag. Where are you going to stay? Your mother's?"

There were tears welling in Gemma's red-rimmed eyes. A single tear streaked down her cheek, leaving a dirty grey line to stand out on her otherwise perfect skin. She let herself out of the booth before more tears escaped.

"I hope you find happiness, Andy" she managed to say despite her anger. As it was with Gemma, however, there came the double edge. "You can pay the check, Asshole."
Andy didn't even watch her leave. Ignoring the stares and whispers of the other bistro patrons, Andy finished his lunch before paying the check and leaving himself.

Andy was alone at the dark table, polishing off his fifth drink while the sixth sat close at hand, ready to chase the last. He'd hit a club after dinner and a few beers with Mark and a couple of other guys from work. He should be feeling at least a buzz by now but he was stone sober. Gemma was leaving him and he didn't care. Freya wouldn't leave him, though. She'd alwaysbe there. She was the true love of his life. He felt it more strongly as the day wore into night. There he sat,downing bottle after bottle of the strongest beer andhe remained sober as the day he was born because he was already drunk with love for his Freya. Gemma be damned. He considered texting her, telling her to clear her stuff out of his house. He was about to start typingit when Mark came back to the table.

"Shit, Andy. You gonna stay there all night? Look at all those young, nubile nymphs just waiting to be conquered. Think of their delicate flowers, just waiting to be plucked," he said, sweeping his arm over the room. "Get out of that bottle and into a pair of those short shorts out there."

"As eloquent as always," Andy said and threw back the last bottle and drained it.

"Go get your dick wet already."

"I'm not loo—". A spectre froze him. Weaving in and out of the crowd. It was Freya, he would have bet anything. He lost sight of her. He got up from the table. Mark was saying something but he wasn't listening. He moved away from the table and down thesteps to the dance floor. He ignored the multitude of writhing bodies and scanned for Freya again. He was beginning to lose hope, thinking he'd gone mad again, that he was dreaming with his eyes open. Then she was there again, across the dance floor looking over her shoulder at him, beckoning him. She disappeared in the crowd again as he pushed his way across the floor.

Finally through the crowd, Andy found himself at the bar. Freya was nowhere to be seen. Of course she wasn't. She's not real, he reminded himself. Feeling defeated, lost and bewildered, he sat at the bar. How had he let himself fall this far? How became so obsessed with a dream that he was seeing her when he was awake? He ordered a drink and nursed it, lost in his thoughts. So lost that he almost didn't notice the woman who took the seat next to him. The first thing he noticed was her flaming red hair, just like Freya's. Slowly, he turned to look at her. She was the picture of beauty, but it wasn't Freya. Disappointed, he turned back to his drink. Then, suddenly, Freya's sweet scent wafted up and hit him hard. He turned and looked at the woman beside him again. She still wasn't Freya. She smiled at him nonetheless, turning slightly to face him. She was stunning, alluring in her own right, but she was not his Freya, not his love.

Impossibly, he felt Freya's lips on his ear lobe, just as he had earlier at the subway station. He could feel her breath, hot on his neck and in his ear as she whispered.

"She is ripe for the taking. Imagine she is me."

Andy smiled his most charming smile and introduced himself to the woman next to him. She probably told him her name, but he forgot it. It wasn't important.

The seduction was easy. He had her back in his house after just one drink. It didn't take much to get her out of her clothes either.

Andy hadn't felt such raw lust since he was a teenager. He went at this woman with wild abandon and she returned every bit of it. They were all desire and lust, passion and want. Their kisses were all tongue and teeth. Andy could feel Freya there, could smell her. He felt her kisses on his neck, her tongue and lips on his ears. She was whispering to him, urging him on.

"Yes!" he heard "More!" He didn't know if it was the woman, or Freya.

As he climbed closer to climax, he felt her more and more real, clinging to his back, pressing her body against his. The woman below him cried out, throwing her head back. She look up at Andy and saw the demon as she materialized on his back. A swirling ash cloud condensed and solidified. Freya grinned down at the woman, showing wicked teeth, her eyes glowed a bright, hellfire red and promised death. The woman's eyes went wide and she would have screamed if she wasn't caught in the throes of orgasm. Freya slipped off of Andy's back and lay beside the couple, watching them ride their wave to its peak. Then she was kissing the woman, moaning, drinking in her pleasure. The helpless woman was caught, forced to ride wave after wave of pleasure, each more intense than the last, building to a deafening crescendo of horrific pleasure. With each wave, the woman became less substantial. Her once buxom figure shrinking and withering to nothing as the succubus drank her essence.

When it was over, Andy rolled off of the husk of the woman and into the embrace of the succubus. Freya wrapped him in her arms, folding her leathery wings around him.

"Now we can be together, my love" she said. "You have fed me, allowed me entry into your world. Your love for me made me real."

"What are you?" he asked before he could stop himself.

"I am desire. I am succubus. I am eater of men."

"You didn't eat me."

"No, I didn't. I would have, but I find I love you." Freya kissed him on the neck and nibbled his ear. "Instead, you will find me victims. You will feed me your lovers." Andy didn't argue, he couldn't, not while she kissed him the way she did. He should have been terrified to be in a devil's embrace, but he desired her more than he'd ever desired anything. They made love beside the empty husk of the woman long into the night. When he woke, she was gone, and so was the body of the other woman.

Over the next few weeks, Andy kept Freya fed with prostitutes. At first, she was satisfied with a feeding every four or five days. Soon though, she demanded more regular feedings. It was at the point now that she required a new sacrifice every night. After the most recent feeding, they were laying together, spent from their love making that always followed, Freya complained of the quality of her meals.

"These women are so empty" she complained. "There is no lust in them, no desire. They are machines, nothing more. I need better prey!"

"These are the ones no one will miss. Everyone cries about how dangerous it is for women, but no one really cares. They forget about it and go back to their lives." Andy stroked Freya's cheek as he spoke, smiling all the time. "If high profile women start going missing, it will draw more attention."

"If you bring me lustful creatures I won't need asmany. You don't want these ones, there is nothing involved in the sex but its machinations, just the act and nothing."

Andy's heart sank to see her pout. He kissed her, bringing a smile to her face once more.

"I want nothing more than to make you happy," he said.

"Then bring me fresh, feeling women. Bring me more like the woman from the club. She was passionate. She was full of desire and sex. I need more like her."

"Your wish is my command." Andy pulled his devilish lover close, kissing her passionately. It didn't take much for the heat to rise between them. Freya was always full of ardour and passion. She was a creature of lust and unbridled sex. Her desires were insatiable. Andy often wondered how she didn't wear him out. He never complained and he wouldn't. He belonged to her completely. He would do anything for her. He would even risk getting caught by the police. He wasn't afraid of the consequences, only that he would be taken away from Freya.

They lay together, entwined in a loving embrace, the earliest rays of dawn's light seeping through the curtains. They were tired from a night of lovemaking. She would soon leave him, going back to whatever hell she came from. Together, they left the bed. They'd said their goodbyes and Andy was about to make for the washroom to clean up. Freya reached for him, taking his hand in hers. She stretched her bat-like wings and wrapped them around him, pulling him close, enfolding him in her full embrace. Her full red lips turned up in her most seductive smile that reflected in her eyes. It melted him to see it. He knew he would do whatever she asked.

"I want to know what love tastes like. I need it." Freya pressed her body into his so he could feel her desire.

And he could. Andy could smell it on her. It was a sweet smell, her natural aroma, more powerful and pleasurable as her ardour rose. He was a soft, pliable thing, like putty in her hands.

She stroked his cheeks and planted small, soft kisses on his face. "Bring me Gemma. Feed me love."

Andy could do nothing but nod his assent. Freya kissed him once more before unfurling her wings and letting him go. She disappeared in a cloud of ash, the smell of sulphur mixing with the sweet scent of her lust and sex in her wake. Andy was left standing alone in his bedroom, a stupid smile on his face. He brushed his fingers over his lips, remembering the last kiss before she left. He went to shower. The long night of sex had left him sticky with sweat and other things. He went with happy thoughts, and began to plan how he could rekindle the romance with Gemma and make the love they shared bloom again. Freya would have her feast.

Andy sat at the table, looking over the wine menu. Gemma hadn't arrived yet and he was beginning to wonder if she was going to stand him up. He supposed he couldn't blame her. What would he have thought if she called out someone else's name in the throes of passion? There was a one bottle minimum for seating at this restaurant, so he had to choose one either way. He settled for a bottle of white (he was going to have either chicken or fish and Gemma didn't eat red meat) when she arrived. He beamed at her and stood from the table, quickly moving around to her side and pulling her chair out before the maître d' could. Always the gentleman. It was one of the things Gemma loved him for, his never ending romanticism. She thanked him and took her seat. He gently pushed the chair in and took his seat across from her. He noted that she wore the cocktail dress he bought her last Valentine's Day along with the matching earrings. It appeared she was pulling out all the stops as well. She wore her hair just the way he liked it, and from the whiff he got when he helped her with her seat, she was wearing the perfume that always got him going. She was either looking to patch things up in a big way or she was rubbing it in his face. Only time would tell. The nagging push at the back of his mind hoped it was the former. The whispers in his head told him it needed to be.

A silence proceeded the seating, neither one knew quite what to say. They were saved when the waiter came by. Andy ordered the one hundred fifty dollar bottle of wine (Gemma's favourite). Gemma leaned forward, her elbows on the table and her chin cradled in her collected palms and smiled.

"You always knew how to treat a lady" she said.

"I didn't know a damn thing about how to treat a lady until I met you"

"And always know just what to say"
"Not always"

Gemma leaned back in her chair, her smile dissolving. She'd hoped to have more of the flirtatious banter before getting to the meat and potatoes. She crossed her arms over her chest and looked at Andy with a blank expression. Andy leaned forward, folding his hands together on the table top.

"I don't know how I can make it up to you, Gemma, or even if I can. All I can do is say how sorry I am for not fighting harder to keep you." He searched her eyes, looking for an indication of how receptive to his apologies she was. He had his foot in the door. Now it was time to nudge it open. "I haven't cheated on you. I haven't even been with anyone since you left." He looked at her, into her, willing her to believe him.

Gemma looked down at her hands. She couldn't meet his eyes under his scrutiny.

"Who is Freya then if you haven't cheated on me? Is she a girl at work you've been fantasizing about?"

"No. She isn't anyone. She doesn't exist. No, listen!"

Andy looked around, making sure he hadn't draw undue attention to them. Gemma had begun shaking her head at the ridiculousness of it all.

"She was just a recurring dream. I know it sounds crazy but it's the truth. She's no one." His eyes told the lie just as well as his lips.

Gemma was still shaking her head.

"Why didn't you tell me about the dreams?"

"What could I say? You would have accused me of wanting other women. You would have assumed I wasn't happy."

Gemma considered his words for what seemed like a very long time. Andy sat, hands still folded on the table, looking her in the eye, imploring her to believe him. His body language said he would have given anything. He was desperate to have her back. That much was true. He played his part well enough that she couldn't have known exactly why and she melted under his gaze, falling for him all over again.

"You're right. That's exactly what I would have thought" she said, frowning at her own admission. "You can't blame me for thinking what I did though."

"No, I can't, and I don't. I'm sorry I let this go on for so long. I should have fought harder. I shouldn't have let you go." He reached across the table and touched her hand. "I miss you."

Gemma returned the touch, moving her fingers over his.

"I miss you too," she said.

The waiter arrived with their bottle of wine. Andy and Gemma locked eyes and smiled at each other while he poured them each a glass. The waiter took their order. They knew what they wanted without looking at the menu. This wasn't their first visit.

They spent the rest of the meal catching up and found they had just as much to talk about as they did six weeks earlier. They laughed and joked, getting to know each other again. It hadn't really been that long, but it seemed like a lifetime. Andy had almost forgotten just how much he enjoyed Gemma's company. She was beautiful and intelligent. She could hold a conversation on a great many topics and that was one of the things that he really loved about her. With all the wine and food he almost forgot his true purpose.

When they perused the dessert menu, Andy turned the conversation to a more flirtatious tone. They joked and made eyes at each other over their desserts and coffee. When the bill came, Andy paid and asked Gemma to come home with him. She wasn't eager to end the evening and agreed. They had both had a little too much to drink for either of them to drive. They called a cab and waited outside the restaurant. The day had been hot and muggy, but an evening rain had washed away the humidity and brought with it a cool breeze. Gemma didn't have a sweater to keep warm, so Andy hugged her instead. They kissed, tentatively at first, then more passionately. They passed the time waiting for the taxi kissing, and reacquainting their bodies. They ignored the stares of people leaving the restaurant or walking by.

Andy took extra pleasure in the seduction, feeling how pleased Freya was. It had proved so easy in the end. Gemma was right, he always did know just what to say.

Discarded clothing marked the trail from the frontdoor of the house to the master bedroom upstairs. Their kissing had continued for the entire cab ride and they barely separated enough to get their clothes off asthey made their way through the house. The passion had been reignited. Andy couldn't deny it. Even having spent the last few weeks with his demonic lover, an insatiable creature of lust and desire, he couldn't help but fall back in love with Gemma. He felt more than a bit sorry that he had to feed her to his dark queen. It wasn't enough to stop him, though, for as much as he loved the woman in his arms, he loved the succubus more.

Andy and Gemma wrestled on the bed, exploring each other's bodies. Neither of them noticed the devil step from the shadows in the corner, taking solid form from ash. They didn't notice the smell of sulphur mixed with the sweeter smell of her pheromones. Freya moved with silky smoothness across the room and stood at the foot of the bed. She watched the couple, feeling their excitement rising. She writhed as she watched, soaking in the sexual energy, her moans joining theirs. She touched herself and found her desire matched the couples'.

Freya crawled into the bed, reaching out to the couple, touching them both, joining in their love. Andy would have been surprised if he could think at all at that moment. He was lost in the sex. With his two lovers in the bed with him, he wished it would never end. They were a mess of tangled limbs, writhing and slithering over each other like snakes in a pit. With much groaning and moaning, screams of passion, they reached the climax.

Andy, like most men, often joked that when he went, he hoped it was while having sex. He didn't actually think it would happen quite like this though. Freya fed from him as he released, drawing first his sexual energies, then his life force. She left him a hollow shell, just as she'd done with the victims he'd given to her. She turned her attention to Gemma, who was looking at the corpse. She reached out and stroked her cheek. Gemma reached up covered the devil's hand with her own, nuzzling, turning her head and kissing the warm palm. They embraced and kissed like long lost lovers. They stopped to take a breath, separating only so far asto do so.

"Was it everything you thought it would be, Freya?'"

"Mmmm, more than I could ever have hope for, my love." Freya spread her wings and gave them a flap as she shuddered with residual pleasure.

"I told you he was wonderful." Gemma pulled herself away from Freya and knelt on the bed. Two demonic horns sprouted, curling from her temples. Bat-like, leathery wings grew from her shoulder blades. The two succubi came together in a passionate embrace once more.

"He loved so unconditionally. It's too bad we couldn't keep him."

They giggled together before resuming their lovemaking. Soon, their moans became echoes andwere gone. There was nothing left but a cloud of ash and the smell of sulphur and sex.

228

Zoe Duff

Zoe lives in Victoria, BC, with her partners, regularly visiting with her eight children and five grandchildren and enjoying the inspirational company of the Eclectic Writers' Boot Camp group, which she facilitates. She has published ten books for adults and children and edited Anthology for a Green Planet, including two of her short stories.

See more from Zoe on her own author's Facebook page (https://www.facebook.com/zoeduffauthor), or follow her on Twitter @polychicbc

"The Lady and the Adventurer" is an excerpt from a novel in the works called *Remembrances Presupposed*. This story is part 1 of a serial novel within the book written by one of the characters, Cora O'Shea.

"Multi-faceted Love" was initially written as writing exercises in the writers' group sessions and fine-tuned for this project.

The Lady and the Adventurer

Once upon a time, in the distant and dreary past, lived a tall, handsome young man named Martin and a lovely young woman of a prominent family named Eliza. Martin and Eliza met at her father's newspaper and publishing company, where they both worked. Their romance began while repairing one of the printing presses late one afternoon. Their flirtatious smiles and handholding, while taking noon walks inthe park near the office, blossomed into steamy kisses in the garden of her family's estate.

Martin spent long hours working on a special project for Eliza's father, and neither man would discuss it. He would disappear for weeks and return apologetic and bearing peculiar gifts that he said were from far-off lands. Her loneliness in these times was lessened somewhat by the attentions of other suitors, but they really just made her miss Martin more. These attentions were something her father seemed to enjoy telling Martin about. The young man grew intolerant of the older man's ribbing, and it eventually caused a rift between the lovers. Angry words, weighted with longing, inflamed their passion, and they consummated their relationship with wild abandon under the privacy curtain of the largest willow tree in the garden.

There were long walks along the cliffs and long evenings cuddled by the fireplace. They always spoke of a future together, yet these moments continued to be interspersed with troubling absences.

Martin was not one to balk at commitment and responsibility. He saw the idea of a wife and family asa natural step and one he anticipated with excitement but hesitated to act upon. Eliza wanted a career and had the drive to make a difference in a world where she was denied much because of her gender. She wanted to learn and grow all of her life and saw their commitment to each other as a foundational expression of love supporting an unlimited buffet of possibilities.

In response to her insatiable curiosity for learning, Martin brought Eliza to a room in the back of a warehouse along the wharf and allowed her to examine his notes and his various inventions. She wandered around the room, studying the drawings and notations and asking very appropriate questions. Martin was continually surprised and impressed with the workings of this woman's mind. She was indeed ahead of her time and perhaps could accompany him on his life's path. Martin loved Eliza more every day. She was the most vibrant and delicious woman he'd ever known, and he had no qualms about sharing his life of adventure with her but knew that it would disrupt the destiny she envisioned.

Eliza and Martin worked together for long hours on what Eliza called their flying carriage. A carriage was built to look like a giant hummingbird witha hot air balloon basket in the belly for passengers. Martin placed controls in the basket that were connected to the speed mechanisms of the wings.A small but powerful steam engine powered those gears and rods. There were also several dials that would set the longitude and latitude of the intended destination.

Martin became aware that Eliza had developed an illness of extreme nausea and fits of vomiting. He encouraged her to stay home and rest and to consult her physician. Eliza would sit and rest more often than usual while they worked, but she would only frown and change the topic of conversation when he asked after her health.

Eliza confided in her old nanny, who advised that nature had its own agenda for the young woman. So it was with a heavy heart and tear-stained face that Eliza next met her love. Martin greeted her with the news that the flying carriage was ready for a test flight and urged her to hurry and join him in the basket seats. All thoughts of babies, the shame of her unwed condition and the expected response of her father flew from her mind as she jumped in and the humming bird's wings began to move.

The machine lifted off the ground and began to spin. Eliza felt bile rise in her throat and covered her mouth. Then there was a blast of light, and the machine began to shake violently. She watched as streaks of light passed by, and bits of debris flew around as if tossed in a wind storm. Finally, there was another blast of light, and the hummingbird spun to a halt with wings slowly stopping.

Eliza leaned out and vomited. Martin jumped out of the basket and helped her out. They looked about with wonder; The warehouse was gone, and they stood amongst rubble. A large metal object flew overhead, followed by several more from various directions. The air was quite thick with a smoky haze. Eliza hadtrouble breathing.

Martin was hopping about yelling, "YES! YES! I did it, you old bastard."

Eliza sat on what once was had been cement steps and tried to catch her breath.

Martin turned to her and handed her a rubber object.

"Put this over your mouth and nose. It will filter out the pollution so you can breathe easier," he said, helping her fit the mask properly.

"Where are we?" she asked.

"2157, I believe."

"21 latitude, 57 longitude?" asked Eliza, trying to pull a map from her memory.

"No, the year is 2157. This is the year I was born," he said, looking into her face and watching her reaction.

"We were born 300 years apart?"

"I did say I was younger."

"How did you end up working for my father? How is this possible?"

Martin told her about his world and the destruction of the planet due to misuse of most resources and war over the acquisition of the remaining ones. He told her about time travel becoming a standard mode of transportation for the wealthy who would holiday at a more congenial point in history. Finally, he told her of his mission to change history and make the development of cleaner and more sustainable energy sources an earlier priority.

"I'm impressed that you want to save the world and have gone to some trouble to do that, but you still haven't told me how you came to work for my father or why you didn't tell me this sooner."

"Would you have believed me if I couldn't show all this to you?" he said, pointing to several flying machines as they passed overhead.

"Probably not," she said, shaking her head.

"In the 1980s, your father's research division, an associated company run by your sister's grandson, does some early work in solar energy applications for air travel but decides it is not as profitable as the more common carbon fuel applications and discontinues the research. I approached your father with the idea of solar-powered steam engines and using tubes of selenium to convert light to electricity a hundred years sooner, hoping to make them the common-place cheaper fuel source. He was fascinated and would drop into the lab unannounced. One day he observed me as I was leaving to travel home. I didn't see him. Several days later, he stole my time machine and had it hidden somewhere. I have been unable to return until I could duplicate the technology and build anothertime machine."

Eliza had many questions, and Martin was thrilled to be free to tell her all she wanted to know. He marvelled at the way his plans had diverted to this wonderful outcome. Eliza was shocked at thecondition of New London and could see clearly Martin's motivation to interfere with history. She rubbed her belly thoughtfully.

"What year would be the most peaceful for a childto be born but yet have the most opportunities available if it's a female child?" she asked.

Puzzled by the question, Martin looked at Eliza, noting the hand on her belly and remembering her nausea. Of course, some people's stomachs just didn't tolerate turbulence, but...

"When?" Martin's face lit up with a grin.

"Six months."

"Sweden, say 2025 for best health care and educational opportunities," he said.

"She or he will be born before you were. Is that too peculiar?"

"Her mother will be just shy of 170 years old. How much more peculiar can we get?"

Eliza nodded.   And so the adventure began.

Multi-faceted Love

Ryan kicked a stone that lay on the sidewalk ahead of him. It bounced along the cement to the edging of a lawn and then back onto the sidewalk. He kicked it again with more significant effort.

"Stupid girls!" he grumbled as he kicked the stone again.

He stopped, took off his ball cap, wiped the sweat from his forehead and replaced the cap. Then, he tossed his backpack onto the lawn and dropped down on the grass beside it.

"What is wrong with you, Ryan?" called out a voice in the distance. "You didn't have to be rude to that old lady."

Sarah ran up to him with her braids flying behind her. She threw her backpack onto the lawn and dropped down beside him. She pulled a bottle of water out of her bag and cracked it open.

"She was just trying to help you make some cash and get her lawn cut."

"Yeah, whatever," grumbled Ryan, "I don't need some old woman's charity."

"Oh, like you have lots of job offers, Mr. Smartypants," said Sarah with a sigh.

Ryan stretched back on the luscious green of the lawn. He studied the scattering of clouds that moved across the sky as it welcomed the sunset.

"Want some water?" asked Sarah, tapping him with her bottle.

"You are only three months older than me, Sarah," he said, closing his eyes and ignoring the tapping. "You don't have to mother me all the time."

Sarah sighed and took another sip of water. She put the cap back on the bottle and slid it into an outer pouch on her backpack.

"You're my brother, I love you, and I want to help you. It wasn't easy going from occasional babysitting to working at the restaurant. No experience is tough to sell." She said quietly. "Suit yourself!"

With that, Sarah rose and strode down the street, muttering to herself. Ryan sat up, opened his backpack and retrieved a bottle of pop. Then, cracking the lid, he stood up and strolled down the street, draining the sweet liquid into his thirsty throat.

Sarah was 18 and more bossy every day. She and Ryan had become siblings when their parents had moved in together ten years before. Sarah's mom, Gina, and Ryan's dad, Ted, had met online in a forum for people practicing polyamory. They began dating not long after that and fell in love almost immediately. Ryan's mom, Sue, and Sarah's dad, Paul, had hit it off more slowly but the two couples had eventually moved into one larger house with their respective children. Sarah was an only child and probably found the change in the size of the household more difficult, but she never complained or took it out on Ryan and his brother, Darren. Ryan had found it confusing as well but had spent his energy helping his younger brother get used to all the extra adults telling them what to do. It had been nice to have an extra mom who liked to bake and an extra dad who took them fishing. Five years ago, they moved to an even bigger house when both moms got pregnant. Kayla and Marie were born two weeks apart and were basically twins, although he wasn't sure which one was bossier. They watched Sarah closely and pretended to be her with their dolls. He and Darren were definitely outnumbered.

Ryan was going to be 18 in two weeks. The household rule was that the children had to have a job by age 18 to provide for college. Sarah was just trying to help him meet that deadline. He knew that, but he needed to push her away and find his solutions. He had had a paper route all through school, and saving for things he wanted was not a new idea. Hard work wasn't a problem either. Cutting old lady Graham's lawn would have been easy. He wantedsomething different. Darren was doing well, having taken over Ryan's paper route. The school year was over soon, and Ryan would be free to explore his own path.

Ryan had also noticed girls paying attention to him in school. Sarah had run interference with the more aggressive girls and while she was popular with the boys in class, too, never responded to them in anything but polite conversation. She preferred tospend time with a clutch of girlfriends. He had his friends too and had been able to spend time with a female friend, Emily, between classes. He liked her, but seeing Sarah talking with his friend Pete yesterday had awakened feelings that had surprised and alarmed him. Sarah was more or less his step-sister, and wanting her to be anything else was just weird. Pete was a good guy. Ryan would encourage him to come around the house and visit with Sarah.

Ryan thought that for both his need for independence and his strange feelings, some distance between him and Sarah was the best idea. In addition, she was mad at him for the moment, which would give him some time to decide what else to do.

A horn honked. Ryan, startled from his thoughts, looked up to see his mom's car pull up beside him. Paul rolled down the passenger's window and asked if he wanted a ride. Ryan nodded and got in the mini van's rear door. Kayla and Marie shifted over so he could get in. Ryan's mom blew him kisses in the review view mirror. Paul chided her to at least pretend to be watching the road.

"Where's your bike?" asked Kayla.

"Home. I have to fix it."

"Do you have to study for exams tonight?" asked Marie, shifting Ryan's backpack on the seat between them.

"Not really. I only have one, and it's next week. Why?"

"Can you play X-box with us? Please? Please? Please?" cried the girls in unison.

When they arrived at home, Ted and Gina were getting out of Paul's sedan, and Sarah was striding purposefully to the front door.

Later that night, Ryan went out to the garage, saying he needed to do some maintenance on his bike but mostly to avoid doing dishes with Sarah. He waspoking around on the workbench for a bolt wrench when his dad opened the door from the kitchen and stood in the doorway watching him.

"So…what's her name?" he said.

"Huh?" said Ryan, finding the wrench and looking up at his father.

Ryan walked over to where his bike stood on its kickstand and bent over to work on the bolt that held the seat in place. Another growth spurt had made the seat too low for him, but, really, he needed a new bike.

"Who's the girl that's got you all sullen and mopey?" asked Ted.

"Sullen and mopey?" repeated Ryan, "Who saysI'm sullen and mopey?"

"Everyone. You're about to be voted off the family island."

"Yeah, well fuck them," grumbled Ryan testing out the new seat height.

"Okay, well, I'm just going to fix your tires with this nail gun, m'k?"

Ted positioned the nail gun over the front tire of Ryan's bike, and half squeezed the trigger.

"Safety is on…Wait! What?"

"Well, if you're going to be self-destructive, we might as well start with the bike."

"I'm not self-destructive. I want a real job, not a bunch of joe jobs. I don't want to start a kid- going-to-college-self-employed thing. I want to move to Vancouver and start a career. It's not about a girl. It's about finding me."

"What about your three college offers for the fall?"

"I need to take a break from school and try myself to check out what's out there for me now, as I am. If I need more, or some different, skills college is there or trade-schools."

"Hmm. You've done some research on this and have a plan?"

"Yes."

"Why move to Vancouver? Sue and Gina won't want you so far away. Neither will Sarah. She talks about being on campus with you."

"Okay, so it *is* about a couple of girls."

Ted took two cans of pop out of the garage fridge and passed one of them to his son. Then, leaning against the workbench, he said, "Spill it, kiddo. I'm all ears."

Ryan sighed and ran the fingers of one hand through his hair. Opening the can, he drank half the contents in one swallow. He told his dad of feelings that began in troubling dreams and now found their way into his daytime thoughts. He was in love with Sarah. They were not related by blood or marriage, but it was still a bit weird. He was happy for her when the boys at school showed her attention. He saw what they saw and was glad that they were open with their admiration. But that confused him even more. If he loved Sarah…like that…romance and sexual responses…should he not want her for himself? Of course, he did, but even more, he wanted her to be happy and loved. He felt a bit sad when she was laughing and talking with one of them because he wished he could love her freely but didn't even go there in fantasy.

"I remember the first time Paul and your mother looked at each other like that," said Ted softly. "I was very happy for Sue and felt joy for her but also but a bit sick in the pit of my stomach. Maybe it is jealousy of a sort. Mostly I guess it was fear that we were setting out on this amazing journey of expanding our love and allowing other people in. Would Paul be good to your mom? Would they be happy together? Gina and I talked a lot about it; she was having some of those same feelings as she watched her husband fall in love with my wife."

"Yeah, that's sort of it. Feeling love isn't what's normal. Not feeling angry jealousy like I should."

"Well, Ryan. Not being monogamous and loving more than one person in my 30's was complex enough but falling in love with someone who is more or less your step-sister at your age is a whole tree full of complicated. No wonder you're grumpy. Is moving to Vancouver supposed to put the brakes on these feelings you're having?"

"No. Yes. Both. I want to get out there and find myself, as I said. But, I think I'd do that better without Mom and Gina, and especially Sarah, holding my hand. I need to grow a set, Dad."

Ted chuckled and drained his can in one last swallow. He nodded.

"But you're scared."

"Yeah."

"I'd think you were an idiot if you weren't scared, and I imagine Sarah's well-meaning pushing isn't as helpful as she'd like."

Ryan shook his head and wiped his hand down his face. He leaned his bike against the wall of the garage and put his tools away. Ted pulled him into a big bear hug and then held him by the shoulders, looking into his eyes.

"I am so very proud of you, Ryan. You are a terrific young man with a huge heart and even bigger dreams. Let's go online and look at jobs and apartments in Vancouver. Paul's company has a Vancouver office, and so does mine. I wonder if we can get you a foot in the door."

Ted slapped Ryan on the back, and they left the garage together.

"I have a friend, Emily, at school who's older brother is living in Vancouver and works for the transit system there. He says I can stay with him for a bit and look for work if I want."

"Oh, that's excellent networking," said Ted, closing the kitchen door.

About Filidh Publishing Authors

We are a group of authors who regularly meet to hone our writing skills, publishing, marketing, and networking with other authors.

Filidh Publishing facilitates the writers' group and hosts Double Dog Dare Open Mic events for unpublished authors to step up to the mic and read from their work for the positive feedback of applause. Likewise, published authors are invited to read from their works, sell copies and build a fan base for that dream career of being a full-time author.

This is the second annual anthology of short stories produced by Filidh Publishing. Most of the authors in this book have stood at the open mic and dared to tell their stories. We hope to inspire you to dare to follow your dreams. We double-dog dare you!!

   For event notices, watch Filidh PublishingOn Facebook at https://www.facebook.com/pages/Filidh-Publishing/167446042117

   On Twitter @filidhbooks
   And at filidhbooks.com